"Jake!"

He grabbed Mariah, hauling her to her feet. Wrapping one arm around her waist, he set out for the relative safety of the woods, not looking back.

She'd been shot. The pain was like nothing Mariah had ever felt.

"I have to stop," she moaned as Jake bent to gather her up to her feet again.

"We can't stop long," he warned.

Letting her go, Jake crossed to the nearest of the trees and tested the connection between the stump and the trunk. The connective wood didn't seem to budge despite the violent shake he gave it.

"It's like a lean-to," he said.

She shook her head, not following.

"I guess you were never a Girl Scout." His eyes narrowed, and she could tell he was wondering how much else about her past he didn't know.

PAULA GRAVES

HITCHED AND HUNTED

TORONTO NEW YORK LONDON
AMSTERDAM PARIS SYDNEY HAMBURG
STOCKHOLM ATHENS TOKYO MILAN MADRID
PRAGUE WARSAW BUDAPEST AUCKLAND

For eHarlequin Subcare, a forum full of tough, dedicated writers who know that success comes one struggle at a time. Keep writing and submitting!

ISBN-13: 978-0-373-69539-3

HITCHED AND HUNTED

ABOUT THE AUTHOR

Alabama native Paula Graves wrote her first book, a mystery starring herself and her neighborhood friends, at the age of six. A voracious reader, Paula loves books that pair tantalizing mystery with compelling romance. When she's not reading or writing, she works as a creative director for a Birmingham advertising agency and spends time with her family and friends. She is a member of Southern Magic Romance Writers, Heart of Dixie Romance Writers and Romance Writers of America.

Paula invites readers to visit her website, www.paulagraves.com.

Books by Paula Graves

HARLEQUIN INTRIGUE

*Cooper Justice
%Cooper Justice: Cold Case Investigation

CAST OF CHARACTERS

Mariah Cooper—When the aftermath of a tornado brings Mariah face-to-face with a nightmare from her past, all the secrets she's been keeping from her husband come to light in the worst possible way—at the end of a gun barrel.

Jake Cooper—He learns about his wife's lies while handcuffed inside a killer's van. Can he put aside his anger and distrust long enough to save himself and Mariah from a dangerous man seeking vengeance?

Victor Logan—He made Mariah Cooper the woman she is, and she repaid him with betrayal, testifying against him after he killed her lover. Now she's back, with a new husband and new identity, and Victor finally has the chance for payback.

Karl—The mystery man may be Victor's ally at first glance, but his clear antagonism toward his partner in crime makes him a wild card who could put everyone's life in danger.

Gabe Cooper—Jake's twin brother begins to worry when his brother doesn't arrive home. Will he figure out what's going on in time to come to the rescue?

J. D. Cooper—A widower still mourning his murdered wife twelve years after her death, he has a stake in what happens to his missing brother that he doesn't even know about.

Chapter One

Mariah Cooper had imagined her death a thousand times in the past four years, but never had she thought she'd be crouched in a motel room bathtub when it finally happened.

"It's going to be okay." Jake's calm voice barely rose above the wind gusts rattling the windows and howling around the corner eaves just outside the motel room. Across the tub, he locked his hands with hers, his blue eyes meeting hers with steady assurance. "Just another tornado warning, right?"

Mariah nodded. Having spent her whole life in tornado-prone areas, she'd responded to hundreds of tornado siren warnings with actions drummed into her head over the years—go to the basement or an interior room, put as many walls between you and the exterior as possible, get beneath something sturdy if possible. Right now, they were on the bottom floor of the two-story motel, and the bathroom was the only place in the room that didn't have an exterior window. The tub had a long steel handle set into the wall to hold on to if things got hairy.

But she couldn't remember ever hearing the wind howl so loudly or feeling the walls shake with each gust.

"It's close," she said, pressure rising in her ears.

Jake's gaze held hers. "It may not even touch down."

On the counter across from the tub, a battery-powered radio kept up a steady stream of chatter from a local station carrying wall-to-wall weather coverage from a television station out of Meridian, Mississippi. The meteorologist was warning people in the Buckley area to get to their places of safety immediately.

"I love you." The warmth of Jake's voice wrapped around Mariah's shivering body. She held his gaze, her heart sinking under the weight of the truth. Jake didn't really love her. He couldn't. He didn't know who she really was.

A crackling boom shook the motel room. The lights surged, then died, plunging the bathroom into utter blackness. Mariah gasped, her fingers tightening over his.

"A transformer blew. That's all." Jake shifted, turning her until she was cradled between his knees, her back against his chest. He wrapped his arms around her, his breath hot against her neck. "Just a few more minutes and it'll be over."

The roar of the wind rose. Cracks and thuds filled Mariah's ears, frighteningly close. Though she closed her eyes against the darkness, as if she could shut it out somehow, the blackness pursued her relentlessly, carried on a sea of destruction encroaching from somewhere outside.

She repeated Jake's promise in her head. *A few more minutes and it'll be over. It'll be over. It'll be over.*

Then, suddenly, it was. The roar of wind fell quickly before dying away altogether, replaced by a steady drumbeat of rain against the windows. Jake began to stir, but Mariah clutched his arms, holding him in place behind her in the tub. They sat quietly, listening to the radio. Only when the weatherman started talking about storm damage reports trickling in from Buckley did Mariah finally move.

"We should see if the truck and boat made it," she murmured, struggling to compose herself.

Jake muttered a soft oath. "Didn't think about the boat."

The power was still out, so Mariah had to feel her way out of the tub and into the main part of the motel room. She'd spotted candles and matches in the drawer of the bureau when she was putting away their clothes a couple of days earlier, so she made her way there and opened the drawer, groping inside until she felt the smooth, cool wax of a candle beneath her fingers. A little more searching garnered the small box of matches as well. She struck a match and touched the tip to the candle's wick. The candle sizzled to life, casting a warm, flickering glow across the motel room.

Mariah turned and found her husband gazing at her, his expression tense but confident.

"Told you we'd make it through." He brushed her arm with his fingertips as he passed her on the way to the front window. He moved the curtain aside and peered out through the rain-mottled windows. His back stiffening, he spoke in a raspy voice. "Good news is the truck and boat are still there. But the shopping strip next door is gone."

Her knees buckling, Mariah stumbled to the end of the bed and sat heavily, her heart pounding wildly. There had been fifteen stores in that strip center. They'd shopped at the drugstore there just that morning. And now it was gone?

She'd known it was a bad idea to come back to Buckley.

THE BAD WEATHER THE night before had bypassed Victor Logan for the most part. A few trees had fallen in the woods surrounding his house, a shanty of a place that was the most he could afford to rent with the little bit of money he'd had left after his legal fees. But he'd seen nothing but a little wind and rain where he lived, despite the tornado siren. And as his old box set television couldn't pick up any channels since the conversion to digital, he hadn't watched the morning news before gassing up his van and driving to town to look for work.

So it was with some surprise that he saw the utter devastation wrought across the small town of Buckley, Mississippi, in the early hours of the morning. Houses with roofs damaged or missing completely. Vehicles upside down, including an eighteen-wheeler wrapped around the concrete piling of an overpass, the trailer split in two, spilling its payload of fresh strawberries onto the roadway. Birds swarmed like winged piranhas, pecking bits of flesh from the berries until the roadside bled red with their juices.

Bodies of farm animals dotted the highway into Buckley, buzzards circling overhead. As he neared town, traffic slowed to a grind due to a roadblock on the highway ahead. The cops must be screening people to be sure they had legitimate business in the storm zone, he realized with a grimace.

He didn't want to talk to the cops, so he turned off as soon as he could, parking in front of a small diner. He'd eaten there a few times. Good food, low prices, and the staff mostly left you alone. Inside, he sat at the counter and ordered the breakfast special—eggs, sausage and a gravy biscuit.

Nearby, a half dozen fellow customers huddled around the diner's small television, murmuring in low tones of horror and concern. Victor could see part of the television screen between their bodies, enough that he got a good look at the devastation in downtown Buckley and on the south side, where the road toward Flint Creek Reservoir had taken a hard hit, wiping out a shopping strip center and several dozen residences.

Victor watched for a moment, his only emotion curiosity. The destruction might open up the job market for him. He was a good mechanic. He could also do construction work if necessary. He just needed someone to look past the black marks on his record. He was starting to get anxious—he'd never been a thief, and he didn't want to become one now just to keep his head above water. Theft was Marisol's crime, not his.

Treacherous bitch.

As he started to look away from the television screen, a face in the crowd behind the male reporter caught his eye. Dropping his fork, he walked closer to the television screen, edging another man out of the way to get a better look.

Marisol. As if his thoughts had conjured her up.

Four years later, she'd changed little, her hair still long and coal black, her eyes so light they looked like pools of silver against the dusky olive of her skin. She gazed straight into the camera, as if looking right at him, and his heart beat a thunderous cadence in his ears.

Her eyes widened and she looked away quickly, as if she'd seen him watching her through the television screen, and turned to speak to a tall, dark-haired man standing beside her. He put his arm around her shoulder and they walked out of the frame.

Victor stared at the screen, barely breathing. He forced himself to listen to the reporter's drivel. The talking head was near a residential subdivision the tornado had nearly wiped out. The people behind the guy were volunteers for the rescue and recovery efforts. More volunteers were needed.

Victor returned to the counter and wolfed down his breakfast. He was on the road within a few minutes.

He bypassed the main highway into Buckley, taking side roads that snaked through the forest and farmlands hemming in the town on all sides. A policeman flagged him down as he entered the affected area.

Victor willed himself to remain calm. He'd done his time. He'd gotten out on good behavior. Seeing his parole officer weekly, as required, and still looking for a job. Plus, he had skills the rescuers could use, didn't he?

He said as much to the policeman who rapped on the driver's side window of his van to ask what business he had in the area.

The cop eyed him a moment before giving a nod. He told him where to park the van and where to find the fire department officer who was coordinating volunteers.

Victor parked where directed and walked to the staging area, a pavilion tent set up in the middle of the road near the tornado strike zone. Inside, volunteers were taking names and handing out bottles of water to those who'd come to support the first responders.

Hers was the first face he saw.

Victor's heart jumped. Marisol was only a few feet away, bending to open another crate of water bottles. She pulled several bottles from the package and set them on a collapsible card table set up in the middle of the staging tent.

She was as beautiful as ever, though time had blessed her, at twenty-five, with a more womanly shape and a leaner, more mature face than she'd possessed at twenty-one. Her dark hair was twisted into a careless braid down her back, humidity giving it a hint of curl in the tendrils around her face. She smiled as she handed a volunteer a bottle, and Victor saw she'd fixed the upper left bicuspid she'd broken as a child.

The man he'd seen her with on TV was nowhere around.

Victor slipped from the tent, not yet ready to be seen. He needed to know why she was here. Was she still living in the Buckley area? Surely not. He'd looked for her in vain as soon as he got out of jail.

Who was the man she'd been with, who'd put his arm around her and led her away from the reporter? Her new lover?

Victor wasn't jealous—he'd never consider sullying himself with her. She'd been an intellectual passion, not an object of sexual desire.

But he hadn't plucked her out of filth to watch her whore her way around Mississippi, either. He hadn't schooled her in the classics, filled her formerly dull mind with the precisions of science and the exquisite mysteries of mathematics to watch her throw her knowledge away on frivolous, romantic dreams of marriage and maternity.

She was supposed to be a different sort of creature, dedicated to knowledge and beauty, not a slave to her baser drives and emotions.

Marisol Mendez had been a great disappointment to him.

JAKE COOPER DRAGGED A large piece of aluminum siding away from the remains of what once had been a split-level home. The tornado had ripped it off its foundation and set it back down sideways, what was left of its front door now facing the house next door, which had barely lost a shingle from its roof.

"Tornadoes." Don, the man helping Jake dig through the rubble, shook his head. "Fickle sons of bitches."

The warning siren had forewarned residents to go to their places of safety. But little could survive the power of an F5 tornado. Somewhere in the twisted bowels of this split-level house, a family of four had been trapped when the tornado hit. Neighbors thought they'd heard shouts for help earlier, but as morning crept toward noon, whoever lay inside had fallen silent.

There was little heavy-moving equipment available in Buckley, Mississippi, to begin with, and all were in use a few blocks over, where the tornado had flattened three full blocks of homes. Here, the tornado had danced along, touching down with random violence, toppling a house here, sparing one there.

"There's a bathroom right around here," Don said as they neared the heart of the house. He grabbed one end of a broken fireplace mantel and tugged. "They'd hunker down there."

Jake grabbed the other side of the heavy mantel and helped Don haul it aside.

"Need some help?"

At the sound of a new voice, Jake looked up. A few feet away, a stocky man with black hair and weather-beaten features watched them, drenched by the steady falling drizzle.

"You bet." Don waved the man in. "I'm Don, this is Jake."

"Cooper," Jake supplied. "Jake Cooper."

"Victor Logan," the stocky man said with a nod.

"We think there are folks trapped in here," Jake explained as they reached the part of the house still standing. The walls here sagged but held.

"This should be the bathroom." Don gestured toward a closed door blocked by the remains of a heavy oak wardrobe.

"We need some sort of leverage," Victor suggested. "Something to wrap around it to haul it out of the way."

"I have rope in my garage." Don lived next door in the house that had sustained no real damage. He headed out.

"We need as much as possible," Victor called after him.

"I don't know how we can set up a pulley." Jake gazed at the cracked remains of the ceiling. The exposed beams overhead didn't look as if they'd hold up if a bird alighted on them, much less take the weight of the wardrobe.

"If the rope's long enough, we can wrap it around that tree there and get enough torque to move the armoire out from in front of the door," Victor said.

Jake gave the man a grateful smile. "You an engineer?"

Victor gave him an odd look. "Sort of. How about you?"

"I'm a fishing guide, here for a tournament at Flint Creek Reservoir this weekend. Guess that's not going to happen now."

Don came back carrying an enormous coil of sturdy nylon rope. "Think this will be enough?"

Victor looked at Jake through slightly narrowed eyes before taking the rope. "Tie this end to the armoire, while I wrap the other end around the tree."

Jake helped Don secure the rope around the heavy wardrobe. "You should stay up here and make sure the armoire doesn't swing into the wall," he suggested when the rope was secured. "I'll help Vic out there pull the rope."

Don nodded his agreement, looking a little sheepish. He was in his late forties and a little on the heavy side; he was already breathing hard and looking worn out from their exertions. Jake was young and fit, and though Victor was at least ten years older, he looked trim and strong, as if he worked out every day.

Jake joined him at the tree, where he was looping the rope around the oak's sturdy trunk. "We ready?"

Victor gave a nod. "Don't let the rope snag on the bark."

"Here." Jake took off his windbreaker and wrapped it around the trunk of the oak, tying the arms together to hold it in place and provide a flat, snag-free surface for the rope.

Victor gave him an approving nod and drew the rope across the windbreaker. "On the count of three."

On three, Jake started pulling his end of the rope, digging his feet into the ground. Two days of rain had softened the lawn, making it hard to stay planted without slipping, but Jake fought for balance and held on. A couple of feet in front of him, Victor grabbed the rope and added his strength.

The rope began moving, slowly but steadily. Within a minute, Jake heard Don call out for them to stop. "It's out of the way! We're in!"

Jake ran back into the house. Don had the door open and was staring into what was left of the bathroom. A gaping hole above let in rain and light to illuminate the debris scattered all around the bathroom, including an enormous jagged slab of mirrored wall that had come to rest against the tub.

"Bill, are you in there?" Don called from the doorway.

"We're okay, I think," came a man's voice. "A few broken bones, some cuts and scrapes, but we're all still kickin'. Just help us get out of here!"

Grinning with relief, Jake looked at Don. "I think the paramedics are all down the road, but the teams at the staging area can reach them by radio—you could go down there and let them know we're going to need help."

"I'll go," Victor volunteered quickly.

"Okay," Jake agreed, a little surprised. Victor had seemed intent on helping out here just a few minutes earlier. "Hey, do me a favor—my wife Mariah's helping out at the staging tent. She's probably worried about me by now. Can you tell her I'm fine and I'll be there soon? Mariah Cooper. She's about five-eight, long black hair, gray eyes, gorgeous—you can't miss her."

"Will do," Victor agreed, an odd light shining in his eyes. He turned and hurried away.

"Ready to do this?" Don asked, waving at the mess in the bathroom trapping the family in the tub.

Jake nodded. Stepping carefully into the mess, he went to work, putting Victor's strange expression out of his mind.

MARIAH WAS CROUCHED BEHIND the water table, opening a new case of bottled water, when she heard a voice as familiar as a nightmare. She stood quickly, banging her head against the edge of the table so hard she saw stars for a moment.

When her vision cleared, she saw a short, muscular man with midnight-black hair flecked with silver standing in front of one of the emergency dispatch stations, rattling off an address. Her heart fluttered wildly before settling into a gallop.

Victor.

As if she'd spoken the name aloud, Victor Logan turned his head toward her. His black eyes gleamed with predatory excitement. Mariah's first instinct was to take flight, but she was trapped between the table and the wall of the tent, other volunteers blocking her means of exit. She could do nothing but stand there, like a bird in a snare, while Victor walked the short distance to her table.

He bared his teeth at her in a horrible smile. "So, Marisol. It's been a while."

She tried to speak but nothing emerged from her throat.

"I have news of your husband. Quite the hero, your husband. Big, strapping, strong fellow. He asked me to tell you he's fine." Victor's smile widened. "For now."

Chapter Two

Mariah clutched the edge of the table, her fingertips stinging from the pressure of her grip. She found her voice, though it came out faint and strangled. "What have you done?"

"I told you, he's fine." Victor picked up one of the bottles sitting on the table in front of her. He made a show of studying the label.

Mariah stepped backward until she felt the canvas of the tent against her back. "What do you want?"

Victor didn't answer, twisting the top off the water bottle. He took a long swig, his eyes never leaving hers.

Mariah clenched and unclenched her fists, eyeing him warily, like a cornered mouse watching a very large, very hungry cat. To her right, the volunteer blocking her exit route moved away, leaving her an unexpected opening.

But before she could make a move in that direction, Victor stepped into the gap, reading her intentions.

She'd forgotten how well he knew her.

He screwed the cap back onto the water bottle. "You haven't told him you were a street whore, have you?"

Though he didn't speak loudly enough for anyone else to hear him, humiliation poured over Mariah in waves of heat. She glanced around to see if anyone was watching.

But they were all too involved in their own efforts to pay any attention to the two of them.

She swallowed the lump in her throat and lifted her chin. "I was never a whore."

"So you say."

She lowered her voice to a growl. "The closest I ever came was living under your roof and letting you manipulate me into being your special project."

"I gave you an education you sorely lacked."

"My education was all part of the game you played with my life." Anger overcame her lingering sense of shame. "It was all about you, all along. The puppeteer, pulling all the strings—"

His brows converged over his long nose. "Apparently I failed to teach you gratitude."

"I'm grateful you helped me when I needed a hand." She softened her voice. "But it should have ended there. It certainly didn't give you the right to kill the man I loved because you could no longer control me."

"It was an accident," he said automatically. The declaration sounded no more believable now than it had when he'd first put it forward as his defense. "My foot missed the brake pedal. I'm very sorry about it."

Hearing his insincere words of regret sickened Mariah. "I want you to leave me alone, Victor. You don't need the trouble, I imagine." He had to be on parole to be out of jail this early. He'd been sentenced three to five years, and he was out after only four.

"Neither do you, I imagine," Victor countered blithely, his mouth curving in a cruel smile Mariah found horribly familiar. "I wonder, which of us will give in first?"

Before she could respond, he tucked his water bottle in the pocket of his jacket, turned on his heel and left the tent, heading out into the rain.

Mariah turned unsteadily back to the table and laid her hands flat on the hard, cool surface, trying to regain her balance. A soft swishing noise rose in her ears, and for a moment, she was afraid she was going to faint.

"Are you okay?" One of the other volunteers put her hand on Mariah's arm.

Mariah nodded, her head beginning to clear. "Yeah. Just a head rush. I'm fine."

"Why don't you sit down?" the woman suggested.

"Actually, I'd like to get some air," Mariah countered, buttoning up her jacket. She pulled a baseball cap from her pocket and put it on, tucking her hair up under the fabric crown. Bringing the bill low over her face, she hurried past the puzzled woman and stepped into the rain.

She started walking east at a brisk clip, toward the subdivision where Jake had gone about an hour earlier to aid a man who'd flagged him down, seeking help for neighbors trapped in their storm-shattered home. He'd been away almost an hour now.

She needed to see him, and not because she needed something familiar and stable to calm her rattled nerves, though that was also true. She needed to know he was okay. If Victor had done anything to him, she wasn't sure how she'd ever live with it.

Not again.

When she found him, she'd convince him to cut short their plans to help in the rescue and take her back home to Gossamer Ridge and their cozy bungalow overlooking the lake. She'd pick up her son Micah from the lake house where he was staying with Jake's parents and never leave Chickasaw County again.

She never should've come back here in the first place.

When Jake had told her he'd signed them up for their first couples fishing tournament, she'd found the prospect exciting. He'd been the one who'd taught her to fish, who'd cheered her improvements and praised her skills every time she muscled a largemouth bass from around a stump or teased a finicky spawning female away from her eggs with an expert twitch of a lure. She'd worked hard to prove herself a good student, to make him proud, and the idea of fishing a tournament with him had seemed like a huge pay-off for her efforts.

She'd been a good sport about having to stay in a motel a half hour north of Flint Creek Reservoir since Jake had waited till the last moment to sign them up and had missed the chance at rooms closer to the lake. Since this trip was their first without three-year-old Micah, she'd even thought the extra privacy, away from the constant presence of their fellow competitors, might turn the trip into the honeymoon they'd never had the chance to take.

Until he'd told her they'd be staying in Buckley.

As she walked, Mariah also scanned the area for any sign of Victor. But he was nowhere in sight.

For a second, she entertained the welcome thought that she'd simply imagined his presence there, in the same place where she'd last seen him four years earlier. The last twelve hours had seemed like a harrowing nightmare rather than reality, as she and Jake had weathered the destructive storm unscathed, only to wake to find a community broken and mourning the tragic aftermath.

Maybe being in Buckley, this beautiful, horrible place she'd thought she'd left behind for good, had conjured up the phantom of Victor Logan after all this time. Or maybe it was the specter of violent death resurrecting long-buried memories, each broken body pulled from the debris and zipped into a body bag a stark reminder of that day, not so very long ago, when she'd watched paramedics back away from Micah Davis's bloody, broken body and declare he was beyond saving.

Mariah faltered to a halt, the memories she'd tried to bury so long ago rising like bile to fill her mind with bitter acid.

Victor had run him down like a stray dog in the street. She'd seen it happen, could now remember every sound, every violent flash of motion and color. If she let it, the memory could play out in an endless, horrible loop, over and over until she felt madness creeping over her in greasy black waves.

She pressed her hands over her face, struggling to push away the memory. She had to keep it hidden, even from herself. It wasn't part of her life now. It couldn't be. Not if she wanted Micah Davis's son to have a good life with the decent man willing to be his father, almost no questions asked.

Jake didn't know anything about her real past.

And if she was lucky, he never would.

"Baby, are you okay?"

She looked up sharply at the sound, half afraid she'd only imagined her husband's voice. But Jake stood a few feet away at the side of an unfamiliar street. She looked around, realizing she'd reached the damage zone more quickly than expected. She now stood across the street from a house the tornado had lifted off its foundation and set back down sideways. The side of the house now facing her had been ripped away, revealing the ruined interior of what had once probably been a nice family home. Emergency vehicles idled at the curb, lights flashing.

"Mariah?" Jake reached his arm out toward her.

Realizing she hadn't answered his previous question, she swallowed hard and shook off the strange sense of unreality gripping her. Drenched and muddy, with a ripped-up windbreaker draped over his shoulder, Jake looked solid and real, dragging her into the present once more. He stepped past the emergency vehicles and hurried toward her.

She met him halfway, throwing her arms around his waist and burying her face into the damp heat of his shoulder.

"What's the matter, baby?" His fingers moved lightly up her spine in a comforting caress.

She couldn't tell him about Victor, of course, but after what she'd seen over the last few hours, she had plenty of ready-made excuses for her shaken state of mind. "This place is just getting to me."

He cradled her face between his grimy hands. "I know. But we're doing good things here." He gestured toward the house. "We just rescued a family of four. Looks like they're all going to be okay, but if they'd been stuck in there too much longer—"

"I know we're doing good things." She looked into his smoky blue eyes to ground herself. Worry faded from his expression when she smiled at him. Sweet Jake, so willing to believe every word she said as long as the lies she spun maintained the little cocoon of safety and comfort they'd weaved around each other.

What would happen to them if Victor ripped it apart with the ugly truth of her real history?

"Could we take a break? Just for a little while?" She looked around them, eyes open for any sign of Victor. But wherever he'd disappeared to, it wasn't here.

"Sure, we can do that." He stroked her hair. "We could go back to the truck for a bit. Maybe dig through the stuff we threw in the cooler this morning and put together an early lunch?"

She smiled at the suggestion, reminded that there was

little that could go wrong in Jake's world that couldn't be solved with a snack. She wondered what it was like to have lived a life so blessedly free of care.

Jake threaded his fingers through hers, tugging gently. She fell into step with him, feeling better as they moved through the busy search-and-rescue area without catching sight of Victor again. They had almost made it back to the staging area on the edge of the makeshift parking lot when a woman came running toward them down a side street that had seemed to escape any of the storm damage.

The woman caught sight of Jake, her eyes fluttering with relief. "Please, my daughter—" She grabbed Jake's arm. Mariah saw that the woman's hands were filthy and scraped raw.

The woman looked terrified. Mariah's stomach knotted in sympathy as she slipped off her own jacket and wrapped it around the shivering, rain-soaked woman's shoulders. "What happened?"

"My daughter—our dog just had puppies and hid them before the storm. We couldn't find them before it hit—" The woman moved her hands away from Jake's arm and grabbed Mariah's hands instead. "There's a creek behind the house. She was afraid they could've gotten down there—I wasn't paying attention."

"Did she fall into the creek?"

The woman was gasping now, from agitation and the exertion of running for help. "All the rain—the bank just gave way—and now she's just hanging there, and I can't get her up." The woman stopped for a hitching breath. "I don't know how long she can hang on—and the creek's up!"

"Show us." Jake was already moving in the direction from which the woman had come. Mariah put her arm around the frightened mother and hurried after him.

The house the woman pointed out was at the end of a cul-de-sac edged with thick, wooded no man's land beyond the backyard. The woman took the lead, rounding the corner of the house and leading them into a waterlogged backyard that ended sharply at the edge of a steep drop-off.

Mariah started toward the creek when Jake stopped her with a quick, firm hand on her arm. "It's been raining for three days straight," he said quietly. "The ground is unstable. You could go down yourself."

From over the edge of the ravine, a small voice cried out in terror. "Mommy, help!"

"Holly!" the frantic woman cried, rushing toward the edge of the yard. Jake caught her, tugging her back to safer ground. The woman struggled against his hold. "She's going to fall!"

"I'll get her, but you need to stay here. We don't want to have to rescue you, too," Jake told the woman firmly.

Mariah put her arm around the woman's shaking shoulders. "We'll get her," she promised. She couldn't blame the woman for her hysteria; the little girl didn't sound that much older than her own sweet Micah.

What if her son were down there, clinging to God knew what, trying not to fall?

"Stay here," Jake told Mariah as she started after him.

"I weigh less. I can get closer to the edge. You can hold on to me," Mariah argued. The little girl was still crying in fear, her voice ringing in Mariah's head until she thought she'd go mad.

What if it were Micah....

Jake frowned, clearly unhappy with her suggestion, but a moment later, he nodded. "We'll see what will work. Just go slowly—the ground could go at any minute."

His warning was unnecessary. The spongy ground beneath her feet grew more and more unstable the closer she got to the edge.

Nearing the precipice, she dropped to her hands and knees, creeping forward until she could see over the edge. The drop-off was sheer and farther down than she expected. The creek that rushed past about ten feet below was swollen and muddy, littered with storm debris that moved at an alarming speed. Five feet below and about three feet to her left, a tiny girl with stringy black curls gazed up at Mariah with wide, terrified brown eyes.

"Help!" Her grubby hands were wrapped around a piece of chain-link fence jutting from the side of the drop-off. It must have been part of an old fence that no longer stood in the backyard. Mariah wondered how securely it was wedged into the muddy bluff face. How much longer could it hold the child?

Jake hunkered down next to her, flat on his belly. His brow creased when he took in the child's perilous situation.

"We could use a rope," Mariah murmured.

"I'm not sure she can hold on long enough to go for one," Jake replied, keeping his voice soft so the child couldn't hear.

"Can you reach her if I hold on to your legs?" she asked.

"I don't think so, but maybe we can haul the fencing up high enough that one of us can reach her."

He slid on his belly until he lay just above the child's precarious spot. Mariah scooted over beside him.

"Holly, my name is Mariah," she called. "This is Jake. Can you hold on tight to that fence a little longer?"

"My fingers hurt!" Holly wailed.

"I know, but I need you to hold on real tight, okay? Jake's going to pull the fence up now."

"No!" the little girl cried in terror. "I'll fall!"

"No, you won't, Holly. Because you're going to hold on just like you hold on to the monkey bars at school. You like to play on the monkey bars, don't you?" Mariah said gently.

Holly nodded, then shrieked as the fencing shifted, dropping her down a half a foot.

Mariah's heart skipped a beat. "Hold still, Holly. Let Jake do it all. You just hold on."

Behind her, Holly's mother was nearing hysterical, calling out her daughter's name in a keening chant.

Jake slid forward until the top part of his torso hung out over the ravine. The dirt at the edge of the drop-off crumbled under his weight, shifting him farther forward than anticipated. He grabbed at the top chain links of the jutting fence to steady himself.

"Jake!" Mariah called, her heart stuttering.

"I'm okay," he said, regaining his balance. He tugged at the chain-link fencing, as if testing its strength. Without the crossbar that would normally give it stability, it was remarkably fluid, since apparently whatever posts had once been connected to the links had fallen away long ago.

Mariah reached down and caught the top edge of the fencing to give Jake more leverage. "Ready, Holly?"

Holly stared up at them wordlessly.

"Let's do it," Jake said.

"Here we go. Hang on tight for me!" Mariah tugged at the piece of fencing, catching her breath as the part of the fence embedded into the earth worked completely loose. The rusty chain links dug into Mariah's fingers as the child's full weight hung from the dangling fencing.

Holly started crying softly.

"I've got you, Holly," Jake called, quickly shifting one hand down until he caught a lower section of the fencing and pulled it up, bringing the little girl with it. Hand over hand, Mariah and Jake tugged the fencing upward, inches at a time, while Holly clung like a baby monkey to the metal links.

"Big, brave girl," Mariah murmured as Jake finally tugged Holly's small form within reach. Letting go of the fence, she wrapped her fingers tightly around the child's tiny wrists.

Anchoring herself in the muddy yard with the toes of her sneakers, Mariah hauled the little girl up to the bluff's edge in one sharp movement, rolling onto her back and bringing the girl the rest of the way to solid ground.

Holly clung to her for a second, until she caught sight of her crying mother. Scrambling up, she raced across the muddy yard and threw herself into her mother's waiting arms.

Mariah pushed up onto her elbows, locking gazes with Jake, whose smile of relief and love brought tears stinging to her eyes. The rain obliterated them before she could blink them away, but the ever-present burn of guilt remained.

She had to tell him the truth. Somehow.

But not here. Not now.

As she eased to her feet, careful of the unstable edge, movement several yards behind the woman and her little girl caught her eye. A man stood at the edge of the property, staring at her with malevolent intensity that even the driving rain couldn't obscure.

Victor.

Forgetting where she was, she took a faltering step backward. The soggy soil beneath her feet trembled under her weight. She stood very still, her gaze still locked on Victor as she waited for the ground to settle enough to dare a step away from the edge.

For a second, she thought it would hold. Then the ground fell out from beneath her, and she was plunging straight downward, the swirling flood waters looming up to meet her.

The last thing she heard before she entered the icy water was Jake's voice howling her name.

Chapter Three

The world was dark and upside down.

Bleak and icy cold, the atmosphere closed in on Mariah in fetid waves, adding to the numbing shock that had already turned her arms and legs to flailing, useless appendages.

She hit something hard, shoulder-first, and realized she wasn't as numb as she'd thought. As pain scorched along her nerve endings into her fuzzy brain, her head burst upward through the murk. She felt the sharp sting of air on her face and drew in a quick, sweet breath.

She saw something large looming toward her at an alarming rate of speed. She almost threw herself sideways to dodge it, until she realized it was a large, weathered tree trunk jutting out into the swollen creek bed. She braced herself, pulling her feet up so that her legs could cushion the impact. Her tennis shoes hit the trunk and she immediately bent her knees to absorb the hit, twisting toward the creek bank so that the rebound would push her toward land.

The ploy worked. Her back slid against the rock-strewn shoreline, shoulders digging into the mud. She grabbed handfuls of mud, anchoring herself, fighting against the swirling current. Her foot touched something hard—a rough boulder embedded in what had once been shoreline, though it was now underwater thanks to the flooding. She planted her feet on the rock, letting it help her stay in place.

Rain was falling in driving sheets, adding power to the flood waters racing past her precarious, half-submerged perch. Her surroundings were unfamiliar, the rushing water and rat-a-tat of rain hitting the canopy of trees above masking any sounds that might have identified her whereabouts.

She heard the sound of something falling toward her. Lying on her back, holding her position with every bit of strength she had, she could only lay her head back and roll her eyes up as far as they could go to see what was coming.

Dark, intense eyes stared back at her from a swarthy, time-weathered face.

Victor.

Her heart stopped so long she thought she'd died. Then it burst to life, racing faster than the flotsam swirling past her. There was nowhere to escape. If she let go, she'd be sucked back into the maelstrom again. She doubted she'd be able to surface for air this time before the water took her completely.

"Interesting situation." Victor edged his way down the incline toward her position on the bank, looming over her like a conquering giant. "So completely at my mercy. You must wonder if I have any mercy left in me, after what you did."

She didn't speak, though anger started to drive out the fear, spreading heat through her cold limbs. What *she* did? All she'd done was tell the truth about what she saw him do.

"Your husband is looking for you. I wonder if he'd care

what happened to you at all if he knew the truth about you."

She sucked a quick breath through her nose, struggling against the urge to lash out at Victor for his cruel taunts. Looking away from him toward the swollen creek, she found her voice. "Of course he'd care. He's a decent human being."

Victor was silent so long that Mariah sneaked another look at him. His eyes were narrowed, his expression contemplative. Was he planning how to get away with another cold-blooded murder? All he'd have to do was pry her fingers away from her death grip on the muddy bank. The water still covered almost two-thirds of her body. Her foothold on the rock wouldn't withstand the rushing power of the flood.

"Mariah!" Jake's voice rose above the water's roar, coming from somewhere above.

A shock of relief rattled Mariah's whole body, so sudden and potent that she nearly lost her grip anyway. She dug her fingers deeper into the mud. "I'm here!"

Victor moved suddenly, reaching down to grab her fingers. She struggled against his touch, terrified.

He twined his fingers through her hair and tugged, sending paralyzing pain shooting through her scalp. "I'm trying to save you, you stupid bitch." He loosened his grip. "He's watching."

Hot tears spilled over her icy cheeks, but she stopped struggling as she spotted Jake scrambling down the incline toward them. She let Victor drag her the rest of the way from the water, scrambling to a sitting position as soon as she felt solid ground beneath her feet.

Seconds later, Jake was there, nudging Victor aside to wrap her in his warm, strong arms, pressing hot kisses against her cheek and brow. Mariah snaked her arms around his neck, relief pouring over her as strongly as floodwater.

"Are you hurt?" Jake held her away from him for a few seconds, his gaze moving over her in search of injuries.

She tested her stiff limbs. She ached from the cold, but everything seemed to be in working order.

"You're going into hypothermia." Jake's search-and-rescue training kicked in. He was an auxiliary deputy back in Chickasaw County, an experienced tracker who'd rescued his share of lost hikers. Mariah knew he was good at what he did.

She glanced over his shoulder at Victor Logan, who stood with statuelike stillness, watching with malevolence that sent a shudder skittering down her spine.

"Just get me to the motel," she said through chattering teeth. "I want to go home."

Jake lifted her to her feet, wrapping his arm around her waist when her knees wobbled upon standing. As she regained her footing, he stopped to look at Victor, whose expression shifted to neutral immediately. "I don't know how to thank you."

Victor's eyes narrowed so slightly, Mariah wasn't certain she hadn't imagined it. "Right place at the right time."

"Well, however it happened, thank you." Jake started up the incline, his grip on her waist firm and supportive.

"Need help getting her up the bank?" Victor asked.

"I'm fine to walk," Mariah said quickly, moving closer to Jake. She forced herself to add, "Thank you."

Her legs ached with exertion by the time they reached the top of the sloping embankment. They were at the end of another, unfamiliar cul-de-sac, in someone else's backyard. Mariah wondered how far the river had taken her. "Where is this?"

"Not sure, exactly. I think it's about five blocks downriver of the other place," Jake answered. "We need to see if anyone's home. You need to get somewhere dry and warm."

"Can't we just go back to the truck?"

"Hypothermia could kill you before we make it back there." Jake half dragged her to the back door of the nearby house and knocked. After a few seconds, a man opened the door and stared at them, his expression wary but not unsympathetic.

"My wife fell into the floodwaters and swept down here from about a quarter mile upriver," Jake explained bluntly. "My name is Jake Cooper and this is Mariah. We were helping with the tornado relief. Mariah's becoming hypothermic—I need to get her out of her wet clothes and warmed up. I'll need blankets."

The man seemed to respond to Jake's firm, no-nonsense tone. "My wife's a nurse. I'll get her. You come on in—there's a bathroom right there." He led them into a spacious kitchen and gestured toward a short hallway. "First door on the right."

Jake closed them in the bathroom. "Brave guy, letting us in. He doesn't know us from Adam."

"Maybe the b-blue lips were a t-tip off." Mariah caught sight of her bedraggled state in the mirror over the sink. She looked horrid, her hair a stringy, tangled mess around her pallid face. Her lips had, indeed, turned a sort of sickly bluish-purple color from the cold.

Jake helped her strip off her muddy clothing and began rubbing her down with towels. In a moment, there was a knock and a woman's voice sounded through the door. "Is she okay?"

Jake wrapped Mariah up in a large bath sheet he'd found in the bathroom closet and let the woman in. "Do you have a fireplace? We need to warm up some blankets."

"Already warming." The woman checked Mariah's pulse with warm, gentle hands. "Not too thready. How's your head—feeling woozy or disoriented?"

"J-just cold," Mariah answered, trying to keep her teeth from clacking together too loudly.

"Poor thing. I would offer an electric blanket, but the power will be out for a bit yet." The woman grabbed a towel from the sink counter and started squeezing excess water out of Mariah's hair. "We should get you somewhere there's power."

"If we can get a ride back to the rescue staging area, I can take her back to our motel. My truck's parked there."

"We'll drive you. We've just gotten back from double shifts at the hospital—Gary's a lab tech and I'm a nurse. We were about to head out there to volunteer ourselves." The woman handed the towel to Mariah. "I'm Sophie. Nice to meet you. I wish it was under better circumstances."

She slipped out of the bathroom for a few seconds, returning with a small plastic bag and a folded set of scrubs. "Let's get you into some warm, dry clothes. These may be a little short for you, but they should fit okay." As Mariah took the surgical greens from Sophie, the woman turned to look at Jake with a critical eye. "You're soaked, too. I'm not sure anything of Gary's would fit you, though—"

"I'm fine," Jake said firmly. "I've been running around so I've stayed warm. Let's just get Mariah back to the motel."

"I'll tell Gary what we're doing." Sophie slipped back out of the bathroom.

Mariah finished slipping on the scrubs. Despite the thinness of the fabric, the clothes were impossibly warm.

"I'd hold you to get you warm, but I'm still sopping wet." A hint of humor threaded through the lingering concern in Jake's voice. Mariah hadn't realized until now just how much she'd missed that lighter tone. It hadn't made an appearance all day, banished by the horrors they were witnessing.

"You can make up for it back at the motel," she promised.

"If you still want to leave town, I understand."

She knew she should tell him no, that they'd stay and help. But the memory of Victor Logan's malevolent gaze was burned into her brain, a reminder of why they had to leave as soon as they could get back to the motel and pack their things.

"I want to go home," she said, hating herself a little.

Within fifteen minutes, they were safely back at the motel. Mariah took a long, hot shower that did wonders for her body temperature, then dried her hair, wrapped herself in a fuzzy robe and finished packing their toiletries for the trip home.

When she returned to the sleeping area, Jake was on the phone. He smiled at her. "Yeah, we're cutting it short here. We may overnight in Birmingham. I'll let you know." He mouthed the name "Gabe." "No, no—she's okay. Just a little chilled."

"Tell your brother I said hi and I'm fine," she murmured, already eyeing the bed, where Jake had laid out warm clothes, including a cozy thermal undershirt and a sturdy pair of jeans. The rest of their clothes were packed.

"So he talked her into it finally? Well, good for Aaron!" Jake grinned at Mariah as she slipped off the robe and started donning her clothing. The appreciative look he gave her as she stripped naked did more to warm her than the thermal underwear. "Tell him congratulations for us. I'll see you later."

"Aaron and Melissa are engaged?" she guessed. Jake's

youngest brother had been trying to talk his girlfriend, Melissa, into marrying him for three months now, but Melissa was too pragmatic to jump into anything. Her history with men had made her a little cautious. To Aaron's credit, he'd been far more patient with her than he was with most things in his life. "Good for them."

"He popped the question on her birthday—talked someone at the high school into letting him borrow the gymnasium and set up their own private prom. Sappy devil."

"Not nearly as romantic as your proposal," she teased, wrapping her arms around his waist. "How did it go again—'Hey, Mariah, wanna get hitched?'"

"If I recall correctly, you were duly impressed."

She rubbed her cheek against his chest, her smile fading. He had no idea how desperate she'd been at that point in her life to find some sort of security and family. She wondered if he'd remember things differently if he knew the whole truth.

Would they even be together if she hadn't been at the end of her rope? She'd never let herself ask that question before, perhaps afraid of what she'd discover.

Beneath her cheek, Jake's sweater was thick and soft. He'd dressed in clothing as warm as her own. She managed a teasing grin. "Got colder than you realized?"

He smiled back at her. "My goose bumps have goose bumps."

"Maybe you should have joined me in the shower."

He pulled her closer, kissing her forehead and threading his fingers through her hair. "You were brave today. You saved that little girl's life."

"We didn't get to tell that poor woman I'm okay."

"We could stop there on our way out of town."

"No, it's not on the way, and it would just interfere with the rescue efforts." Mariah already felt guilty enough about leaving all those poor, suffering people behind. But she couldn't risk seeing Victor Logan again. "Besides, she probably took her little girl to the hospital to be checked out."

"Maybe I should take you to the hospital, too. You're still shivering."

She couldn't tell him her chills had more to do with the cold-eyed man who'd been seconds from tossing her back into that swollen creek before Jake arrived.

Not yet. Not until they were safely away, back in Gossamer Ridge, with Jake's big, capable family surrounding them.

But when they got home, she was going to tell Jake the truth. The whole sordid story.

It had been a mistake to create a fictional back story for her own life. Jake deserved better, and she was strong enough to face her past.

She'd survived seeing Victor again, hadn't she?

Barely, a cowardly voice whispered in her ear. *You barely survived with your life.*

THE SECRET TO GETTING away with something, Victor knew, was to look as if you know what you're doing. In his case, it was simple enough; Victor actually knew his way around the underbelly of a truck. He'd been a mechanic since the age of sixteen, working in garages and repair shops across three states. He'd been bitten with the wander bug at an early age. With his skills as a mechanic to sustain him, he began a twenty-year sojourn across three states to find where he belonged.

Twenty years to figure out he'd never belong in this world full of cretins and imbeciles who were more interested in expanding their wallets and waistlines than improving their minds. It had taken Alex to show him the truth: he was better than all those people he'd spent his life trying to impress.

After that, he'd lived his life as he wished, taking the jobs that would best accomplish his particular needs at the time. Alex had been generous, as well, sharing his wealth with Victor in exchange for Victor's keen eye for opportunities.

Alex's money had bought Victor the toolkit he was using right now under Jake Cooper's Ford F-150.

Victor had followed Marisol and her husband from the disaster scene, seen him forced to park the truck many slots down from their motel room because of the bass boat hitched to the back. It had been easy enough for Victor to park nearby, bring out his tools and act as if he was there on business.

Victor was slender enough to slide easily under the truck and snip the serpentine belt without engaging the car alarm. He left just a thread of belt intact. It would snap within a few miles, and not long after that, the engine would start to fail.

He pushed out from under the truck and walked purposefully back to his van, securing his tools on the floorboard behind the front passenger's seat. He stepped into the van through the side door and closed it behind him, quickly stripping out of his wet, soiled coveralls.

Then he left the parking lot and set up a couple of blocks down the service road. Cooper would have to drive past him to get to any of the three interstate access roads.

And Victor would be ready.

MARIAH WAS TOO QUIET. It reminded Jake, uncomfortably, of their first interactions three years ago. She'd showed up one day, looking for work, and his sister Hannah, always a sucker for a stray, had talked their parents into hiring the shy, pretty young single mother for the clerical job at the booking office of the marina and fishing camp the family ran.

Jake had found her stunningly beautiful from the start, but her quiet demeanor had almost nipped their relationship in the bud. He'd always preferred vibrant, fun-loving girls with lots of energy and lots of sass. Mariah's subdued, self-contained calm seemed just the opposite.

But as she revealed her past in painful little snippets over the next week, he began to understand that what he'd seen as self-possession was really lingering sadness at the loss of her husband, Micah's father. He'd apparently died young in a tragic car accident, leaving Mariah pregnant and alone. He'd had nothing to leave them, forcing Mariah to fend for herself and her child with her own resources.

Pity had turned to sympathy, and sympathy to infatuation. By the time she'd finally agreed to go out with him three weeks after they met, he was halfway in love. Their first kiss two dates later sealed the deal for him, and it hadn't taken long to convince her they were meant to be a family.

They'd eloped to Gatlinburg within two months of their first meeting. He'd never doubted his snap decision to marry her, or be the father to her adorable son Micah, who'd just turned three in December.

But at times like this, when she went quiet and insular, he was reminded there were still things about her history he didn't know. Things he hadn't thought important.

But what if they were?

Mariah looked up, her forehead wrinkling a little as she caught him watching her. "What's wrong?"

He tried to shake off his doubts. "Nothing. Just—you're so quiet. You're not feeling worse, are you?"

She flashed an unconvincing smile. "Still cold, I guess."

He started to reach behind him to the bench seat when a sharp snapping sound caught him by surprise. Almost immediately, the steering wheel grew stiff under his hand, and the engine power dropped precipitously.

He fought the unresponsive steering wheel, bringing the truck to a shuddering stop at the side of the road. The engine idled unsteadily for a few seconds, then died. When he tried to crank the engine again, the starter struggled to engage.

"What happened?" Mariah's eyes widened with concern.

He reached over to touch her hand. He felt her hands trembling. "I think a belt must have broken," he reassured her, although he'd checked all the belts and hoses before they left home. "I'll take a look."

The rain had slacked off, thankfully, only a light mist falling now. Jake slipped the hood of his windbreaker over his head and hurried to the front of the car. He raised the truck's hood and looked inside.

The serpentine belt was hanging loose, snapped in two.

He uttered a low curse, wishing he'd taken his brother J.D.'s advice and packed extra belts for the journey. But J.D. was a control freak—who ever listened to his advice about things? He was the kind of guy who'd pack a parka for a trip to Florida, just in case another ice age hit unexpectedly while he was there.

He closed the hood and pulled out his cell phone, but his phone couldn't find a signal. They were in the middle of nowhere, thick, piney woods flanking them on both sides. He'd taken a side road rather than the main thoroughfare, which was still clogged with traffic in and out of Buckley. He wasn't sure there were even any houses within a square mile.

"What is it?" Mariah joined him in front of the truck.

"Belt broke."

"What do we do now?"

Jake was about to suggest walking back to Buckley, but the sound of an approaching vehicle distracted him. He saw a white van coming up the road toward them. "We flag down this van and see if he can take us into town."

He started waving at the van, which slowed as it came nearer. A mild glare off the windshield obscured the driver until the van was nearly on them.

It was Victor, the man from the tornado zone.

Mariah's fingers closed around Jake's arm, digging in. "Let's just walk—"

He looked away from Victor to Mariah, who was gazing up at him with wide, terrified eyes. "What is it?" he asked.

"You folks need a ride?" Victor called out. Jake saw Mariah's gaze shift behind him. Her face blanched white.

He turned, following her gaze, and saw Victor Logan standing in the open side doorway of the van, arm outstretched. In his hand, Victor held a large black Smith & Wesson semiautomatic, its barrel leveled with the center of Jake's forehead.

"Let me rephrase," Victor said, his voice cold and steady. "Get in the van or I'll kill you."

Chapter Four

Jake wanted to make a move on him. Victor saw it in the younger man's watchful eyes, the taut set of his muscles as he backed up against the interior wall of the van. Victor had spent the last three and a half years honing his ability to spot danger coming from miles away. A man his age and size didn't survive prison without knowing how to avoid danger.

When it could be avoided. And sometimes, it couldn't.

Victor shook off the grim memories before they could paralyze him. He had work to do, and he wasn't about to drop his guard with Jake Cooper.

Marisol was Victor's protection. Jake would weigh any move he might wish to make against the danger his action would pose for her. It had taken only seconds for Victor to read the situation and train his weapon on Marisol rather than Jake.

He hoped it was enough to keep Jake at bay.

"I'm waiting," he said aloud, not hiding his impatience.

Marisol's hands shook as she followed Victor's directions, fastening the plastic cuffs around Jake's wrist, then hooking the cuffs through the metal clips attached to the inside of the van. The clips had been there when Victor bought the delivery van used, probably to secure stabilization ropes for transporting furniture or other large items.

He'd spent many long hours contemplating the various ways those clips could come in handy one day. He just hadn't anticipated the day coming quite so soon.

"Sit over there." Victor flicked the barrel of the gun toward the long wood bench that lined the opposite side of the van. Marisol glared at him with eyes full of equal parts hate and fear as she did as he demanded.

"What do you want with us?" Jake asked, not for the first time. Over his head, he flexed his wrists, testing the plastic cuffs, his movements subtle.

Victor wasn't worried that Marisol had tried to trick him by leaving the cuffs loose. She knew better by now than to cross him. She knew the consequences.

"Marisol, do you have an answer for your husband?"

"Why do you call her Marisol?" Jake's curious gaze slanted toward his wife.

She looked over at Jake, fear and guilt written across her face as plainly as words. Slowly, she turned her gaze to Victor, and for a brief, breathtaking moment, rage and hate eclipsed her earlier fear.

Victor's breath froze in his throat.

Then fear took over again, and she dropped her gaze.

Victor breathed again, crossing to her side. He almost felt sorry for her.

Almost.

He secured her wrists, taking care that the bindings were tight enough to pinch. Drinking in her soft gasp of pain, he took strength from the sound. *Who has the power now, Marisol? Who's in control this time?*

Hooking her cuffs to the clip over her head, he stepped back, surveying his handiwork. The man was glaring at him, impotent rage shining in his eyes. But Marisol kept gazing down at the floorboard, her whole body slumped with defeat.

If only Alex were here, Victor thought with pride. If only he could see what Victor had done, how he'd taken the gift the universe had given him and turned it to his favor, things between them would be different.

With a sigh of regret Victor turned his back on his captives and slipped into the driver's seat of the cargo van. He cranked the engine, and the van roared to life.

"I'm going to tell you a story," he said over the engine noise, slanting a look toward the rearview mirror. In the reflection, he saw Marisol's head snap up, her gray eyes blazing hatred as they met his in the mirror. He fed off her hatred, his voice gaining power. "It's the story of a lying, stealing, whoring piece of street trash who had the chance to change her entire world. And failed."

THE PLASTIC RESTRAINT cuffs were painfully tight. Jake had hoped Mariah would leave them loose deliberately, had even tried to communicate that plea with his eyes as she cinched his wrists together, but she'd left him little slack to work with. Still, they were plastic and, unlike the disposable cuffs he and other deputies were used to handling back at the Chickasaw County Sheriff's Department, these cuffs were cheaply made. He had a small butane lighter in his front pocket—one he'd bought the day before at a convenience store near the motel when weather reports made it clear they might be experiencing long power outages due to the coming storms.

If he weren't hanging like a side of beef from the overhead clip, he might be able to burn through the cuff in no time. All he needed was the right opportunity.

In the driver's seat, Victor began talking, his voice deep and surprisingly cultured. Jake had noticed it before, back at the disaster site, but the smooth, educated accent was even more noticeable now, echoing through the cargo van.

"She was given everything, asked for nothing but her effort and her loyalty."

Jake glanced over at Mariah, trying to catch her eye. But she was glaring at Victor, her color high. "Shut up!" she shouted. "You lying son of a bitch!"

Jake stared, shocked at her outburst. Mariah was one of the most gentle, even-tempered people he knew. He'd never heard a curse word pass her lips in the three years he'd known her.

"Would you prefer to tell the story, Marisol?" Victor asked, apparently unfazed.

"Why do you keep calling her Marisol?" Jake repeated before Mariah could speak again.

"Would you like to answer that, Marisol?"

Jake looked across the van at his wife, who continued to stare at their captor, her eyes ablaze with unadulterated hatred. "Mariah?"

Her gaze turned slowly to meet his, and the rage died, leaving only despair in its wake. Tears welled and spilled over her bottom lashes, trickling down her cheeks.

His gut knotting, Jake waited for her to tell him Victor was lying, that he was crazy. But she just looked down at her feet, teardrops splattering the muddy metal floorboard between her shoes.

"Your wife has kept secrets from you, Jake." Victor's voice nearly quivered with anticipation.

"Is that what this is all about?" Jake asked, his gaze still fastened on Mariah's downturned face. "You knew each other before? What—he's Micah's father?"

"No!" Mariah's gaze flew up, not to Jake but to Victor's reflection in the rearview mirror.

"Micah?" For the first time since he forced them into the van, Victor sounded uncertain.

Jake didn't answer, keeping his eyes on his wife as he struggled to understand. So whoever Victor was to Mariah, he didn't know about her son. And clearly, she didn't want him to.

And neither did Jake. Even if he *was* Micah's father, no way in hell would Jake let him anywhere near the little boy he thought of as his own son.

"Do you have a child, Marisol?" Victor asked in a strangled tone that caught Jake by surprise.

"I meant her husband, Micah," Jake lied quickly as he saw Mariah's face turn deathly pale. "Are you his father? Mariah told me his parents didn't approve of their relationship."

Victor laughed. "No."

"Victor killed Micah," Mariah growled, her voice dark with old pain.

Jake had heard that sound, more often than he liked to remember, in the early days of their courtship and marriage, but he'd thought she was past it now, moving forward into their new and promising life together.

Clearly, he'd been wrong. In so many ways.

"It was an accident." Victor's flat tone was unconvincing. "I paid for my mistake."

"You killed him so I couldn't be with him," Mariah countered fiercely. "That was your twisted idea of disloyalty to you. Is that why you're doing this now? Are you going to kill Jake, too?"

"If all I wanted was to kill your latest lover, he'd be dead already," Victor said calmly.

"Easy to talk big when you've got the gun and your opponent's trussed up like a turkey, little man." Jake watched Victor for a reaction.

Victor ignored the taunt, but Jake noted that his back stiffened at the hard words. The older man turned his attention back to Mariah, his dark eyes focusing on her in the mirror. "You made things very difficult for me. You ruined everything."

"*You* ruined everything," Mariah spat back at him. "You're the one who couldn't let me go."

"Your name is Marisol?" Jake asked quietly, partly to defuse the escalating tension but mostly to distract himself from the twisting in his gut. He knew that Victor wanted him to feel disgust and betrayal at Mariah's lies. He could see very well that Mariah wanted—needed—him to trust her.

All Jake knew was that she wasn't going to die on his watch.

Mariah lifted her face slowly. He could see she was struggling to meet his eyes. "My name is Mariah Cooper. I changed it legally three years ago, and then changed it when we married. Marisol is a different person from a very different time and place."

"Not so different," Victor said flatly. "Same old liar."

Mariah's lips pressed to a thin line as she shot a glare at Victor. She turned her gaze back to Jake, her expression tense. "I know I have a lot to explain. I'm so sorry. But nothing you're hearing now changes who I am."

Jake wanted to agree, to wipe the fear and dread from her expression. But he wasn't going to lie to her.

At the sight of his indecision, her expression fell. She turned back toward the window, her profile outlined with despair.

Jake looked into the rearview mirror and saw Victor's black eyes watching him. "Where are you taking us?"

Victor's only answer was a slow, enigmatic smile.

AT LEAST WE'RE STILL ALIVE.

As mental pep talks went, the silent chant running through Mariah's head wasn't exactly a source of inspiration. She and Jake were still alive, yes, but for how much longer?

And what did Victor intend to do to them in the meantime?

She knew firsthand what he was capable of doing. She'd seen the way he'd aimed his old green Caddy at Micah Davis as he walked across the campus service road to reach Mariah on the other side. There'd been no hesitation. No tap of the brake.

He'd known what would happen to Micah's body when the Cadillac's nose slammed into him at forty miles an hour. He'd counted on it.

She'd often wondered, later, if he knew she'd be there to witness Micah's murder. For reasons she hadn't admitted to herself until it was too late, she'd kept Micah a secret from Victor, as much as she could. Victor had been ambivalent about allowing her to attend college in the first place, as if he were somehow insulted that she needed to learn things that he couldn't teach her.

His possessiveness—not of her body but her mind— should have been a warning of what would come.

From her position in the belly of the windowless van, all she could see of the world outside was the relentless blur of greens, browns and grays through the front windshield. Victor was driving them into the woods. She didn't want to think about what would happen when the van finally stopped.

She dared a glance at Jake. His eyes were angled forward, slightly narrowed, his expression intent. He probably thought they still had a chance to get out of this mess alive. She didn't have that illusion.

All she had were regrets.

The van slowed, the wheels skidding a little as if they'd hit a patch of mud. Mariah held her breath, willing the van to pick up speed again. She didn't want to believe this was the end of the road.

But the van rumbled to a full stop, and Victor cut the engine. The resulting silence was almost a shock, until the faint sound of rain outside filled the void.

Mariah looked at Jake again, her gaze drawn by a need she couldn't quantify. Was it love? Fear? Shame?

Jake's eyes remained on Victor as the older man stepped through the space between the front seats and entered the cargo area. As he crossed to Mariah's side, Victor kept his eyes on Jake. "Don't be stupid. Either of you."

He released Mariah's cuffs from the hook over her head. She dropped her hands in front of her, flexing her aching shoulders. "Just do whatever you want to do to me and let him go."

Victor laughed. "You're the one who brought him into this, Marisol. Without even telling him the truth about what he was signing on to. You'll just have to live with the consequences of your deceit." He motioned with the gun. "Unhook him."

Mariah pushed unsteadily to her feet, wincing as the plastic cuffs dug into her wrists. She crossed to Jake, fighting hot tears as his blue eyes lifted slowly to meet hers.

She couldn't read his emotions. She probably didn't want to know what he was thinking right now anyway.

She unhooked his cuffs and took a step back so he could stand. She felt something hard dig into her spine between her shoulder blades.

"My gun is directed at her heart," Victor said. "One wrong move and I will pull the trigger. Are we clear?"

Mariah almost made the move herself, just to get it

over with. He wasn't going to let them out of here alive. Prolonging fate was nothing but torture.

Jake's eyes bored into hers. For a second, she saw real emotion there, burning like a flame. "Nobody's doing anything stupid," he said aloud.

She heard his message loud and clear.

Behind her, she heard the click of a latch and the swoosh of the side door of the van sliding open. Cold, damp air poured over her body, eliciting a shiver.

She heard the sound of Victor's footsteps retreat behind her. A moment later, he spoke, his voice a few feet away. "Turn around, Marisol."

She turned to look at him, loathing burning in her chest, fueled by every fear, doubt and regret she'd ever had in her life. Victor stared back at her, his eyes coal-black and cold. There had been a time when she'd thought he was her friend. Maybe her only friend. Certainly her mentor.

But that was before she'd discovered what he really was.

He motioned at the wet grass below with a sharp jerk of the gun barrel. "It's a short jump."

She dropped from the van to the ground, gasping a little as her foot slipped on the wet grass. Almost immediately, Jake was right behind her, his solid body stopping her fall.

"Step away from her," Victor growled.

Jake stepped back but remained close enough that she could feel his warmth despite the cold drizzle falling around them.

Victor had stopped the van a few feet beyond a small one-story bungalow built of river stone and wood siding that might have been white before weather and age had rendered it a drab, lifeless gray. A wooden porch extended the length of the house, covered by a sagging aluminum awning that seemed incongruous to the rest of the structure.

"Home, sweet home," Victor murmured with a humorless grin.

Quite a comedown from the nice split-level he'd rented in Buckley proper, Mariah thought. She supposed he'd lost the lease while in prison.

Still, for a while, it had almost seemed like her home.

Inside, the sparsely furnished living room smelled musty. The darkness of the interior multiplied as Victor closed the door behind them, shutting out the gray light of the rainy day.

Victor didn't bother turning on the light. He nudged Mariah's back with the barrel of the gun. "There's a door ahead, just to the left. Open it and turn on the light."

Jake, who walked ahead of her, did as Victor commanded. He stopped in the doorway and looked back at Victor, rebellion written all over his face. "We're not going down there."

Mariah peered around him and saw what the bare lightbulb revealed—a narrow stairway leading down to a shadowy basement.

Stained cement floors. Exposed water pipes, cold and damp with condensation. The odor of mold and grime, filling her lungs with each breath. Darkness as deep and black as hell.

Her head swimming, Mariah stretched her bound hands forward, trying to find her balance.

Jake caught her hands in his, his fingers warm and strong. She gazed up at him, grounding herself in his gaze.

"You know I hate basements, Victor." Her voice came out low and raspy. "Put us somewhere else."

"Down the stairs," Victor said flatly. "Go."

Jake's fingers tightened on hers. He spoke in a voice so quiet she could barely hear him. "You can do this."

He led the way downstairs, his head high and his back straight. Mariah took strength from the sight of him moving slowly, steadily down the steps in front of her, a solid wall to stop her fall if she should lose her step.

The basement was as dark and fetid as she'd feared, but she could feel Jake's warmth just in front of her, and some of her panic eased.

Victor turned on the light, another grimy bare bulb hanging from a wire overhead. Mariah blinked against the sudden illumination, her eyes adjusting until she saw that the basement was somehow even more depressing and dank than she'd imagined.

Victor directed them to the far wall, where water pipes curved along the grubby stone foundation. Jake muttered a low curse. "Just had these lying around?"

Peering around Jake, Mariah saw what he'd spotted—a set of handcuffs attached by one cuff to the pipe.

"I like to be prepared." Victor waved toward the rickety-looking bench in front of the handcuffs. "Sit down, Jake. Mariah, I believe you've had some experience with handcuffs. Please put them on your husband." He spat out the last word with pure contempt.

The paralyzing fear that had gripped her the moment he walked into the tent earlier that day had finally begun to fade, replaced with a simmering rage that twisted her gut into hard, fiery knots. *Give me a chance to stop you,* she thought. *Just one chance.*

"Would you rather be in the cuffs?" Victor picked up a pair of rusty wire cutters and motioned for her to come to him with the barrel of his gun. "That can be arranged."

Mariah eyed the wire cutters. Could she get them away

from him? They wouldn't be much of a match against a gun, but any weapon was better than none.

She let him snip through the flexible cuffs, making a show of rubbing her chafed wrists. But the second he turned toward the table to replace the wire cutters, she made her move, grabbing the heavy tool from his hand.

He stared at her in disbelief as she took a swing, slamming the wire cutters against the side of his face. They connected with a jarring thud, and Victor staggered forward.

Mariah tried to back away as he loomed over her, but her feet tangled in something on the basement floor. Windmilling her arms, she tried to keep her balance, but Victor's body crashed into her, driving her backward to the floor.

The breath whooshed from her lungs and the world turned into a chasm of smothering pain.

Chapter Five

Mariah's attack was so unexpected, Jake couldn't move for a few endless seconds. Like a movie playing out before his eyes, the next sequence of events unfolded in slow motion and crisp focus. Victor lurching forward. Mariah losing her balance. Their bodies colliding, falling to the floor in unison, Mariah momentarily pinned beneath Victor's stocky form.

As the sound of her gasping efforts to breathe broke through his paralysis, he started forward, forgetting he was still shackled until the flexible cuffs bit into his wrist.

Training, Cooper. Use your training.

He located the weapon first. Victor still held the Smith & Wesson, his fingers closed around it where it lay on the floor. Conscious and moving around, Victor was still a threat. To handle that threat, Jake needed full mobility. He had to lose the cuffs and might never get a better chance than now.

He freed the butane lighter from his front pocket, flicked it on and held it under the plastic cuffs. The flame came too close to his wrist, searing his skin and forcing a hiss of pain between his teeth, but the cuffs melted. He snapped free of them just as Victor pulled Mariah to her feet.

Jake palmed the lighter, expecting Victor to turn the gun on him again to make sure he was still under control.

He'd underestimated the laser focus of Victor's rage.

A torrent of profane insults flowed from the man's lips as he dragged Mariah toward the stairs, not giving Jake a second glance. Caught back on his heels, it took Jake a second to get his own feet in gear and follow, reaching the stairs as Victor and Mariah neared the top step. Mariah was moving in Victor's grasp, Jake saw with relief, drawing shallow, whooping gasps of air as if the wind had been knocked from her in the fall.

Her eyes met Jake's as Victor hauled her through the basement door into the living room and disappeared from sight, leaving the door ajar. Taking the stairs two at a time, Jake burst into the living room behind them. Victor and Mariah were already halfway outside, Mariah fighting in earnest now.

By the time Jake reached the porch, Victor had pulled her most of the way to the van. He still held on to the Smith & Wesson, swinging it freely at his side as he held Mariah in the fierce circle of his other arm. But when he caught sight of Jake, his arm whipped up and squeezed off a wild round.

The bullet flew wide, slamming into the front wall of the house about three feet from where Jake stood. He dropped to the porch and rolled off, landing behind the sparse cover of a rusted rain barrel that stood just beyond the rickety eaves. Rain splashed in the half-full barrel, pouring down from the angry gunmetal sky.

"Jake!" Mariah's cry rose like a howl of wind, flowing over and around him, filling his ears with its pressure.

He dared a peek around the rain barrel in time to see Mariah slam her head back into Victor's face. The man staggered back into the side of the van, losing his grip on Mariah. She stumbled and fell to the ground, landing in the muddy grass.

What happened next unfolded with the same, surreal quality of the events Jake had witnessed in the basement. Mariah rose to her feet. Victor's arm came up, bringing with it the large black Smith & Wesson, too close to miss this time.

Jake struggled against the mud sucking at his shoes and tried to reach Victor before he fired off another round. But he was too far away.

The gun barrel jerked. The crack of gunfire split the air. And Mariah went down again.

Jake felt an impact in his chest as if he'd taken a bullet himself. But he kept running toward her, heedless of Victor, of the gun now swinging to aim at him.

A snapping sound, oddly distant, echoed through the damp area around them. Behind Jake, Victor let out a howling stream of invective.

Jake looked at him, certain he'd be staring down the barrel of the gun. But Victor was pressed flat against the van, holding his hand clutched against his chest. Blood stained the fabric of his gray cotton windbreaker, trickling from beneath his fingers. The gun was nowhere in sight.

Another odd snapping sound. The right front tire of the van popped like a balloon, air hissing out of the shredded rubber. Someone was shooting from the woods, using a sound suppressor.

Mariah's fingers closed around the front of Jake's shirt. Her quicksilver eyes reflected fear and pain, but also a fierce, feral intensity that spurred him out of his momentary shock.

Survival instinct screamed at him to run.

He grabbed Mariah, hauling her to her feet. Wrapping one arm around her waist, he set out for the relative safety of the woods, not looking back.

THE UNEXPECTED GUNSHOT had come from the east, where the land rose sharply to form Bitter Creek Hill. From higher ground, a decent shot using a good rifle with a scope could have hit Victor with a little luck and good visibility.

Only a crack shot could have hit the barrel of his 9mm and ripped it out of his hand at that distance, especially using a sound suppressor.

The shot had not repeated, and Victor had unpeeled himself from the side of the van and raced into the house, which would provide at least a semblance of cover. Inside, he also had supplies—bandages and ointments to treat his torn palm.

The rifle bullet had hit the weapon, not his hand, but the wrenching force had dragged the grip safety across the flesh of his palm, ripping it open. Now that Victor had the bleeding under control, he saw that the cut wasn't as deep as he'd feared. He cleaned the graze, applied ointment and closed the wound with butterfly bandages. He wrapped his hand in gauze and surgical tape and headed back out in the rain.

He made it as far as the top step of the porch when a tall, well-built young man walked around the corner of the house, a rifle with a sound suppressor attached to the barrel propped against one shoulder and the carcass of a rabbit flung over the other. He smiled a greeting and came to a stop in front of the stairs, effectively blocking them.

"Karl," Victor breathed.

The man he knew as Karl Avalon smiled more widely, his expression open and friendly. But Victor wasn't fooled. He had already experienced Karl's treachery firsthand.

He was also pretty sure Karl Avalon wasn't his real name.

"Nice day for hunting," Karl commented.

"Hunting season's over," Victor growled.

"The rabbits don't know that," Karl said with a shrug.

"I was doing a little hunting of my own earlier." Victor tried not to look at the rifle, but he couldn't stop himself. The Remington 700 was fixed with an expensive long-range scope. Nothing that rabbit hunting would require.

"I saw."

Victor was tired of the verbal game. "Why did you stop me? They can ruin everything."

"Not everything." Karl arched an eyebrow.

"So what is this? Sabotage?" Victor shot the younger man a sharp look. "Haven't you done enough of that?"

"You were reacting in anger, not good sense. You wounded the girl. It won't be easy to make it look accidental now. But you'll have to try." Karl's gaze moved away from Victor toward the mangled Smith & Wesson still lying on the grass a couple of yards from the van. "Dispose of that. Somewhere the authorities won't think to look. And they will look, once they figure out the woman's connection to you."

Victor stared at Karl through narrowed eyes. How had he figured it out? He knew about Marisol, of course— Victor had made the foolish mistake of letting his prison pen pal in on far too many details of his former life. But even Victor hadn't known, until he walked into that disaster relief tent, where Marisol had disappeared to.

He wondered now if Karl had found her long before she showed up at the tornado damage zone earlier that day. Karl was working with Alex now, and Alex certainly had far more resources than Victor ever would.

"I gave you a second chance to get this right, Victor." Karl glanced toward the woods where Victor had last seen Marisol and her husband running for cover. "You know these woods. They don't. Make it look like an accident this time. Alex doesn't need the scrutiny. Neither do you." With a short nod, Karl started walking away, heading down the dirt track that would eventually wind its way back to the interstate access road.

"That's it?" Victor called behind him. "You're leaving me to handle this on my own?"

Karl turned, wearing a puzzled look that Victor didn't buy for a moment. "Are you incapable of handling it on your own?"

Victor pressed his mouth into a tight line. He didn't dare answer. Karl already had enough to tell Alex as it was.

Karl gave a brief, satisfied nod, then turned and started walking again.

THE PAIN WAS LIKE nothing Mariah had ever felt. Intense, like the worst contraction in the world, but burning instead of aching. And the blood saturating her sweater was oozing out in sufficient quantity to feel heavy, dragging her down on one side even as she struggled to keep up with Jake's zigzagged dash into the woods.

Her feet felt sluggish, moving at a different speed from the rest of the world. A hidden root snagged her toe, sending her sprawling forward to land on her injured side. The impact sent darts of pain flying like shrapnel through her. She tried but failed to bite back a cry of pain.

"I have to stop," she moaned as Jake bent to gather her up to her feet again. "I can't—"

He gave her a look of pained regret but gave a nod. "We can't stop long," he warned.

She shook off the blinding panic and made herself think through the pain. She was bleeding too much. They hadn't even looked at the wound yet, afraid to stop even a moment as they dashed away from Victor and whoever had been lurking in the woods above, shooting down at them. She found her voice, though it came out in a raspy gasp. "I'm bleeding too much. Probably leaving a trail."

He checked under her jacket, his eyes widening with alarm at the amount of blood. Fighting the wet bulkiness of the bloodstained sweater, he tried to lift her garments to check the wound, but the fabric clung to the bloody gouge, rocketing pain through her side again.

His brow furrowing, Jake looked around them. Mariah wasn't sure what he was looking for so determinedly, but a few seconds later, she could see from the look of triumph on his face that he'd found it. He put a firm arm around her waist, careful not to touch the wound. "Stick with it a few more seconds and we can rest."

She didn't have the energy left to ask where they were headed. She just leaned her cheek against his shoulder and tried her best to keep pace as he half walked, half dragged her several yards deeper into the dense woods. He came to a stop in front of a pair of fallen pines that had criss-crossed each other, the snapped trunks lying at an angle, still partially attached to the broken stumps by a couple of slabs of rough bark and the outer rings of the interior pulpwood. Stump, trunk and ground formed a triangle that rose at its highest point to about six feet where the tornado winds had found the tall, slender trunk's weak spot.

Letting her go, Jake crossed to the nearest of the trees and tested the connection between the stump and the trunk. The connective wood didn't seem to budge despite the violent shake he gave it.

"It's like a lean-to," he said.

She shook her head, not following.

"I guess you were never a Girl Scout." His eyes narrowed, and she could tell he was wondering how much else about her past he didn't know.

"You think we can make a shelter out of it?" she guessed.

"It seems pretty sturdy—the winds couldn't snap these trees completely in two. I can pick up fallen limbs and use them to create a roof, of sorts, for us. It'll shelter us from the rain and also make us harder to see if anyone comes looking for us while I'm examining your wound." He held out his hand toward her.

She placed her fingers in his palm. He closed his hand around hers and led her under the makeshift gable the fallen pines created. Clearing out the top layer of wet pine needles at the foot of the tree, he revealed another layer of needles that were barely damp at all. "Sit there."

Hurting too much to offer to pitch in and help him, she sank to the ground and pulled off her rain-drenched windbreaker. The waterproof material had kept her mostly dry, at least from the rain, though her own blood drenched her side as surely as the storm.

She pulled her sweater over her head, ignoring the ache in her side as her skin stretched to accommodate the movement. With both garments lying on the ground beside her, the damp chill of the woods seeped through her cotton thermal undershirt, making her shiver.

Or had she lost enough blood that she was going into shock?

Jake returned with arms full of broken pine boughs. As he layered them over the tree trunks, adding to the natural foliage already providing cover, Mariah was surprised how much of the murky gray daylight Jake's contraption blocked from her sheltered area.

She'd known, because she'd heard the stories he and his brothers told, that all the Cooper kids had grown up roaming the woods around the lake as if it were their own private playground. She knew they were good trackers, experienced woodsmen, but until this moment, she'd been too much of a city girl to really understand what that meant.

Jake knew how to protect them because he'd probably been fending for himself in the heart of untamed nature his whole life, in one way or another. She had been camping with Jake before, but only in a cozy, relatively high-tech tent, not a makeshift shelter in the middle of rain-soaked woods with a vicious killer and God only knew who else trying to find them and shut them up.

She'd let his penchant for jokes and his lighthearted personality blind her to the fact that he was a deeper, more capable person than she'd thought.

Somehow, she hadn't counted on that fact.

Jake finished building the shelter and settled onto the ground beside her, shrugging off his own jacket. Leaning closer, he gently tugging at her blood-soaked thermal shirt.

The fabric pulled at her torn flesh again with a searing rush of agony. She bit back a cry.

"I'd say go ahead and scream," he murmured, "but that's probably not a good idea."

She nodded, breathing swiftly through her nose as he tugged the fabric the rest of the way from the wound. He pulled out something she couldn't quite see from his front shirt pocket. A second later, a tiny flame ignited, shedding pale gold light across their tiny den.

"It's not as bad as it looks," he murmured, though the expression on his face wasn't reassuring. "There's some scorched fabric we'll need to clean out of it—"

She shuddered at the image his words conjured. "There's nothing clean about this place."

"I know." He dug in the pocket of his discarded jacket and pulled out a folded blue bandanna. "It's not sterilized, but I haven't used it since it was washed. It's the best we can do until we get to civilization."

"When do you think that might be?" she asked, gasping as something he did to her wounded side sent pain arcing along every nerve ending in her body.

"I don't know this area that well." Jake's head came up, his blue eyes meeting hers. "This is your neck of the woods."

"Not really. I never came out this far. I stayed in Buckley proper. Never went much farther than Southern Miss up in Hattiesburg," she said between gritted teeth.

"Is that where you met Micah?"

She released a shallow breath as the bandanna scraped across her wound again. "Yes. He was a graduate student—teaching assistant. I was auditing a freshman-level Western Civilization course he was helping the professor teach."

"Love at first sight?" There was nothing sarcastic in Jake's tone, to her surprise. He'd have been well within his rights to doubt anything she'd told him before. She'd certainly lied about most of it.

But she hadn't lied to him about her love for Micah. "Not at first sight. But close."

"You weren't married, though."

"No. We planned to marry. But then he died."

"Hold this." He took her left hand and pressed her fingers against her injured side. She hissed with pain but held the folded bandanna in place while he stripped off his shirt to get to the plain white sleeveless undershirt below. He seemed to fill the confined space of their tiny hideout, his broad shoulders and powerful chest reminding her of the solid strength that had attracted her to him in the first place.

She'd met Jake on one of the lowest days of her life. She'd gone to Gossamer Ridge, Alabama, in search of hope. She'd found none. The job she'd wanted was taken already. Her search for permanent safety against the threat of Victor had reached a dead end. Alone in a strange town, surrounded by people who didn't know who she and her small son were and probably didn't care, she'd spotted the now hiring sign on the wall of the Cooper Cove Marina's bait shop and walked headfirst into Jake Cooper's broad, muscular chest.

Was it love at first sight? A treacherous voice in her head whispered a challenge.

It hadn't been. She was still grieving her murdered lover, wrapped up in trying to provide security and happiness to his tiny son. She hadn't realized then that grief, like guilt and shame, never really goes away.

"Did you change your name to get away from Victor?" Jake's question dragged her back into the present, where the afternoon was beginning to give way to twilight, and the temperature was dropping ahead of an approaching cold front.

"Yes," she answered.

"What was it before? Marisol what?"

"Mendez."

"You told me you grew up in Texas. Is that true?" He tore his undershirt into long strips, the ripping sounds impossibly loud. Mariah knew that pursuers probably wouldn't be able to hear the noise over the driving rain outside, but she still cringed a little at each tear.

"I was born in Beaumont. Grew up in Houston. I left when I was sixteen."

Jake tied a strip of cotton undershirt around her waist to hold the bandanna bandage in place. "Runaway?"

"Emancipated minor."

One dark eyebrow arched as he looked up at her. "So Mariah Miller Davis's happy childhood was a fabrication?"

"I never knew my father. My mother was strung out on drugs most of the time I was with her. Which was off and on for fifteen years, until the Texas Department of Family and Protective Services decided she'd had enough chances. The foster families were sometimes good, sometimes not so good. But I never stayed with any of them for more than a couple of years at a time."

Jake finished tying off a second strip of undershirt to her makeshift bandage. "Why not?"

"My mother kept convincing her case worker that she'd finally gotten the drugs under control. Or the drinking. Or whatever her addiction of the day might be." Mariah struggled against pain, both the searing agony in her side, and the older, deeper ache of her shattered childhood. "Finally, when I was fifteen, the courts refused to give her custody of me again. I was free to be adopted."

"At fifteen?"

"I was way beyond adoptable by then," she conceded. "There was one foster family I hoped might take me, but they'd moved to another state at that point. I didn't know where they went." She remembered the Fonseca family with fondness. They'd taken her in the first time, when she was just five, and kept her for almost two years before her mother had gotten herself together enough to petition for custody reinstatement. With them, she'd known for the first time what a real family felt like.

"So you had yourself declared an emancipated minor?"

"Yes."

Jake fell silent and sat back, shrugging on his shirt. He was playing his emotions so closely to his broad chest that she wasn't sure whether he really cared what had happened to her in the past or if he was just making conversation at this point.

The Jake Cooper she knew, the one who'd swept her

into a whirlwind romance three years ago, dashing away every roadblock she'd put in place to keep herself from being sucked into his exuberant undertow, always seemed to wear his big heart on his even bigger sleeve.

What if that man had been a lie all along? Hadn't she wondered, almost from the beginning, if the easygoing man she married, the man who never asked the hard questions even when he should, was just a mask covering his real identity? Hadn't she worried that Jake, like Victor Logan, had a darker side that might strike at the worst possible moment?

What if this watchful, wary stranger was the real Jake Cooper?

Of all the things that had frightened her over the past twelve hours, looking into Jake's cold eyes and seeing only her reflection mirrored back was the most terrifying of all.

Chapter Six

Her name was Marisol Mendez. She was twenty-one years old and the happiest woman in the world because Micah Davis had asked her to marry him.

Standing at the corner of Stadium and West Fourth, waiting for her brand-new fiancé, she was already indulging in daydreams about the kind of wedding she wanted, the house they'd rent or maybe even buy, once Micah earned his master's degree and got the job she knew he'd get, because he was wonderful and brilliant and destined for stunning success in life.

She wasn't used to hope. Life to this point had given her little reason to anticipate the future. She often found herself looking over her shoulder, certain someone would come along to tell her she hadn't earned her good fortune.

But that was before Micah.

The only fly in the soul-soothing balm of her current happiness was Victor. Her mentor, her friend, the man who'd saved her life and given her opportunities she'd never dreamed she might have, wasn't happy that she was marrying so young.

She couldn't make him see that she was only young in age. Her soul was ancient and growing older by the day. She'd lived a lifetime, most of it hellish and depressing, by the age of sixteen. She'd lived a whole other life of despair *after that, until Victor had saved her from arrest, refusing to press charges when she'd picked his pocket on a New Orleans street three years ago. A misunderstanding, he'd assured the policeman.*

He'd taken her in that very day.

She owed him everything—her life, her newfound thirst for knowledge, his patient schooling in every subject she'd missed over her nomadic young life—literature, history, the sciences and math. Victor had introduced her to a world of learning. In a way, he'd led her to the love of her life. He had inspired her to audit a history class at the university.

He'd come around. He wanted her to be happy, didn't he?

She spotted Micah coming across the street, the early May breeze ruffling his thick dark hair and plucking a sheaf of papers from his arms. She laughed softly, watching him chase the errant papers with the boundless, joyful energy of an overgrown puppy. He was only a couple of years older than she was, but in so many ways, he was a child in comparison, blessed with a happy family and a life that had been golden from the very beginning, born into a home where he was wanted and loved.

Maybe that's why he'd accepted her, with her faults and failings. In Micah Davis's world, evil was a theoretical construct, not a reality lived with every hour of the day.

He caught sight of her and threw up his hand in an enthusiastic wave, losing his grip on one of the papers he'd gathered up. The wind took the sheet toward the street, and Micah chased after it.

The intersection was clear, and pedestrians had the right of way. Micah scooted into the crosswalk, his attention wholly focused on the elusive page. But Mariah, whose eyes were on her lover, saw what he never would:

an old green Cadillac flying down the road, the engine gunning. No brakes. No slowing.

She knew what would happen. She'd played this scene over in her head thousands of times since that nightmare of a spring afternoon, and it never changed.

Victor never put on the brakes.

Mariah struggled to escape the nightmare's grasp before the tragic climax. But she knew she wouldn't succeed.

The nightmare always won.

MARIAH'S RESTLESS SLEEP drew Jake's attention from the woods barely visible through the narrow gap in the pine boughs covering their lair. Outside, night crept closer, aided by dark rain clouds that wouldn't clear the area until after midnight.

He and Mariah should have been out of here hours ago. But she'd fallen asleep while they watched for pursuers, and considering the pain she must be in, he was loath to wake her.

She had begun stirring a few minutes earlier, her breathing quickening. She shifted restlessly, wincing as the movement pulled at the wound in her side. But he knew it wasn't her injury that caused her disquiet.

It was Victor.

Her nightmare wasn't new. For the first year of their marriage, bad dreams had disturbed her sleep regularly, often jarring her awake. God knew how many times he'd held her shaking body until she quieted enough to go back to sleep. She could never remember the dreams, or so she claimed. Given the other lies she'd apparently told him over the past three years, a fib about her dreams was a minor sin in comparison.

The nightmares had begun to go away around the middle

of their second year together. By their second anniversary, they were gone, seemingly never to torment her again.

Until now.

Mariah jerked awake, sitting up in a rush. Her head thumped against one of the branches that formed the roof of their lair, and she released a soft grunt of pain.

Jake reached out to steady her. Her whole body flinched at his touch.

"It's me," he said quickly, gentling her with a light stroke on her arm.

Her eyes focused on him, huge and dark in the low light. "We're still in the shelter."

"Yes, we are."

She pressed her hand against her injured side, grimacing with pain. "What time is it?"

He checked his watch, pushing a button to light up the dial. "Six-thirty."

"Morning or night?" Alarm pitched her voice up a notch.

"Same evening as before."

Her anxious expression didn't clear. She struggled into a full sitting position, grunting softly with pain. "You shouldn't have let me sleep. We need to get moving."

He stopped her as she attempted to rise to her knees. "Moving where?"

"We can't stay here."

"I think we're better off here than out there for now," he countered firmly. "It's already near dark, and we don't know these woods—"

Panic colored her voice. "Victor will find us."

"He'll look," Jake agreed. "But if we stay right where we are, we should be safe enough. He hasn't found us yet, and unless he has a bloodhound or something—"

"He hates dogs," she said flatly. "Fears them, anyway. He thinks they're dangerous and dirty."

Jake thought about Rowdy, his brother J.D.'s hound-mix dog, as good-natured and loving a canine as ever lived, and almost laughed aloud.

Only there was nothing to laugh about, was there?

"I don't know the way out of these woods. Do you?" he asked as she settled back into a sitting position.

She shook her head, her fingers dropping to her side where the bullet had grazed her, worrying the hidden bandage.

"Is your side hurting?" he asked.

"Just twinges."

He couldn't tell if she was lying. "Let me take a look."

"Later," she said firmly. "Jake, I'm not sure we should try to stay here overnight. It's only going to get colder, and I'm already freezing. We're in wet clothes—"

He was halfway dry now, his windbreaker having taken the brunt of the rain. His jeans were still damp, but not unbearable. Then again, he hadn't fallen into an icy river earlier that day.

"We'll curl up together. Share body heat." As soon as he made the suggestion, an image of his body wrapped around hers flooded his mind and inflamed his senses. He'd always loved the way she felt, spooned against him in the aftermath of lovemaking, every inch of her flesh warm and soft where their bodies touched.

Even now, even here, even with all the lies that had passed between them since their first meeting, there was a part of him that wanted nothing more than to strip naked and bury himself in the heated silk of her body.

He opened his eyes, staring at the muddy, uneven ground beneath them. He breathed in the damp, chilly air and searched for the tattered scraps of his self-control.

"How much do you hate me?" Mariah's question caught him by surprise. He looked up to find her watching him. Despite her drenched, bedraggled appearance, she was still the most beautiful creature he'd ever seen. But in the dark depths of her quicksilver eyes, he saw an ancient, simmering pain he'd never seen before. Or maybe it had been there all along, and he'd never let himself take notice.

He was beginning to think there was a lot about her that he'd never let himself see, never wanted to see, because he might have to make hard choices.

"I don't hate you," he said, and meant it.

"But you're angry."

He shook his head. "Not now. I'm just—" He paused, struggling to find words for the strange numbness that had settled in around his heart like an icy fog. "I'm just trying to figure out what to do next." His reply was also the truth, though it didn't quite answer her question.

"I should have told you from the start." In her voice, he didn't hear conviction, only a question.

"Yes," he agreed, with the conviction she lacked. "Did you think I was going to look down on you because of your past?"

"Wouldn't you have?"

He realized he didn't have an answer. He didn't think any less of her now for her rough, hardscrabble past because he'd lived with her for the past three years, knew that she was a woman of intelligence, compassion and strength.

Would he have given her a second look if he'd known about her troubled past from the beginning? Would he have taken a chance on someone who might turn out to be a bad risk? He'd like to think so, but he knew the answer was probably no. He avoided complications in his life. Always.

Her chin lifted. "Would it help to know the truth now?"

Jake felt a little spark of life in the cold region around his heart. He just wasn't sure if it was anticipation or dread. But at least it was a sign of life, for good or for bad.

"Okay, tell me," he said, settling next to her to lend her his body heat. But even as she snuggled closer, the movement seeming more instinctive than deliberate, he wondered whether he could believe anything she had to say.

VICTOR FINISHED DIGGING the second slug from the siding near the front door and tucked it in the pocket of his jeans. He was pretty sure he'd hit Marisol with the last shot he was able to get off, though the wound hadn't kept her from disappearing into the woods with her husband.

There were traces of what might be blood on the slug, but it had flattened on impact with the house anyway, so he couldn't tell if he'd hit bone. Probably not, since she was still able to run. The bullet had probably grazed her side before slamming into the clapboard siding, not far from where the first bullet he'd fired had hit.

He was lucky the bullet wasn't still in her. Now he could dispose of it, just in case the police came looking.

At least she and Jake had run into the woods to the east, away from the road. They'd never find their way out of the woods before nightfall, which was fast approaching. The smarter thing to do would be hole up somewhere, get their bearings and try to hike out by sun up.

Either way, they'd probably be wandering around for a while trying to find a way out. He knew the creek circled this patch of land, so they wouldn't be able to go far in any direction before hitting the creek. And if it was still up as much as it had been earlier, they wouldn't be able to figure a way across it.

He had time to gather all the evidence that would prove they'd been anywhere near these woods and dispose of it. Starting with Jake's truck and boat.

He fixed the van's tire and drove about halfway down the muddy dirt track to the main road, parked and walked the rest of the way, hoping someone hadn't already called in the broken down truck with the boat hitched to the trailer in back. With relief, he discovered the truck was still there, apparently untouched. No sign of a warning ticket on the front windshield to suggest a patrol car had spotted it and flagged it for illegal parking.

After replacing the snapped belt, he opened the truck cab and found the keys still in the ignition, to his relief. In the excitement of taking Marisol and her husband hostage, he'd forgotten to pat the man down for the keys or weapons.

He was making too many mistakes.

When he tried the starter, the engine coughed a few times but soon roared to life. He planned to drive it about five miles up the road, where a dirt track turn-off led to the edge of a bluff overlooking the swollen floodwaters of Bitter Creek. It would mean a long walk back to the van in the rain, but it was worth the effort.

He couldn't go back to jail again.

As he reached for the gear shift, movement in the side mirror made him jerk with surprise. The driver's door opened and Karl stood there, a baseball cap shielding his face from the drizzle. "What're you doin', Vic?"

Victor hid his irritation. "I thought you'd gone already."

"Nope." Karl shook his head. "This isn't your car, Vic."

"Thank you, Captain Obvious."

Karl's smile faded. "You're going to leave those bags in there when you dump it?" he asked, nodding toward the bench seat behind the front seats.

Victor looked back and saw a couple of soft-sided suitcases lying on the bench seat. "I was going to make it look like an accident," he said aloud to Karl, hiding the fact that he hadn't thought about luggage at all.

"Nobody's going to buy that he'd drive his truck into a creek and just float away."

Victor's annoyance level spiked. "So what would you do, Junior?" he asked, taking pleasure from Karl's obvious dislike of the nickname he'd just used.

"I'd go with a variation of the truth." Karl leaned his head farther into the truck cab to take a look around. "Someone carjacked them, shot 'em and dumped 'em in the woods. Stole the truck, then thought better of trying to get rid of such a nice vehicle, so they took what they could find inside and left. Carjackers wouldn't leave the luggage. That would be easy enough to haul with them."

"Why should I listen to your ideas?"

Karl snorted. "Because you need all the help you can get. You screw this up, it could blow back on more than just you."

"Then why did you stop me from killing them both back at the cabin? Why would you screw around with me that way?"

Karl's expression went deadly. "Because I could."

Victor understood the implicit threat. It chilled him to his marrow.

If he tried to cross Alex and Karl, his life would be over.

Karl's face softened, his eyes going oddly gentle. "Come on, old man. I'll dump the truck for you down the road a

ways. You grab the bags and haul 'em back to your van."
He held out his hand as if to help Victor from the cab.
Victor saw that he was wearing latex gloves.

Victor wasn't.

Karl's lips curved in a knowing smile. "Don't worry.
I'll wipe it down for you before I leave it."

Victor got out and started to reach for the bags on the
bench seat, but Karl waved him off. "I'll get them for
you."

Stewing in humiliation, Victor waited for Karl to hand
off the bags. He tried to keep his voice neutral, free of his
roiling emotions. "You should stay away for a while."

"Oh no. I'll check back tomorrow. Make sure you have
your situation under control." Karl got into the truck and
put it into gear. Victor had to step back to keep from being
sideswiped as Karl drove away.

The bags were heavy to begin with, heavier still by the
time Victor reached his van and hauled them inside for the
trip back to the cabin. His earlier chill had fled, replaced
with a boiling rage that burned from his insides out.

How have I come to this? Victor wondered, climbing
behind the wheel of the van.

Marisol.

It's Marisol's fault.

He would make sure she paid. Tonight.

MARIAH STRUGGLED TO KEEP her eyelids open. Jake had
been right about one thing—body heat was going a long
way toward driving out the chill, even if it couldn't do much
about the constant, burning pain of her bullet wound.

A moment earlier, he'd wrapped his arm around her
shoulder, pulling her even closer to his solid warmth, and
for a few seconds, she could think about nothing but the

way he smelled, like pine needles and motel soap from the showers they'd both taken before checking out.

Those showers seemed like a lifetime ago.

"Your mother was an addict?" Jake's voice jarred her, jangling her nerves. She'd almost dozed off in the middle of her thought.

She sat up straighter. "Coke at first. Then when she couldn't afford that anymore, crack. I was lucky—she was clean when she was pregnant with me. I could easily have been a crack baby at birth."

"Where was your father?"

"I'm not sure she ever knew who he was," she answered, that part of her past no longer able to cause her any shame. Micah had taught her that much—that she couldn't be defined by anything that had happened before she came kicking and screaming into the world. "She slept with a few guys back then. Whoever would have her."

"What about your grandparents?"

Sweet Jake, she thought, so sheltered by his own rock-solid family. He probably assumed everyone had family to fall back on just because he did. "I never knew them. My mother said they kicked her out of the house when they caught her in the back seat of a car with her boyfriend at the time. She said she was only sixteen."

"You don't believe her?"

Mariah shook her head, wishing her mother's constant betrayals didn't still have the power to sting. "She lied all the time. About everything. Even when the truth would have served her better."

Jake's answering silence felt like an indictment. She'd lied when the truth might have served her better, too, hadn't she? She could have told him the truth from the beginning. And not just about her past, but also why she'd really gone to Gossamer Ridge, Alabama, in the first place.

No. She couldn't be certain she was right about her suspicions, and the Cooper family had already suffered enough—

Next to her, Jake's body suddenly jerked to full alert. His head cocked to one side, he touched his fingertips to her lips, his eyes glowing with alarm in the dying daylight filtering through the pine boughs above them.

"What is it?" she mouthed, not making a sound.

Quietly, he shifted position to look through a narrow space between the broken limbs sheltering their hideout. He drew back quickly, alarm sparking in his eyes.

Silently, she scooted closer to the side of the shelter and peered out into the gathering gloom.

Not twenty yards away, Victor Logan crept through the woods, a revolver in one hand and a flashlight in the other. At the moment, the flashlight beam was dark, perhaps to hide his position as he hunted his elusive prey.

Mariah couldn't hold back a tiny gasp.

Victor froze in place, his head swiveling until he seemed to be staring right at her.

An icy chill shuddered through her that had nothing to do with the cold.

They'd just run out of time.

Chapter Seven

His breath trapped in his chest, Jake watched Victor take
a couple of steps toward their modified lean-to. From a
distance, the construction wouldn't look suspicious, but if
Victor came much closer—if he turned on the flashlight
in his left hand and fanned it toward them—he wouldn't
be fooled by the camouflage.

In front of him, Mariah's body shook so hard her teeth
chattered. Afraid the noise might draw Victor even closer,
he wrapped his arms around her, drawing her back against
his chest. "It's okay." His voice was little more than a soft
exhalation.

Victor stopped, his head slightly cocked, as if unsure
what he was seeing. Jake's pulse hammered in his throat,
but he forced himself to focus. If Victor found them, Jake
would have to protect Mariah and disarm the man from
a position of extreme disadvantage. He needed a way to
even the odds.

Taking his eyes off Victor just long enough to scan the
interior of their hiding place, Jake considered the options.
A large stick? Not much good against a gun, but better than
nothing. However, moving any branches inside the shelter
to retrieve a sturdy limb would certainly give away their
position.

Then he spotted a small, hardy-looking branch lying

near the back edge of the shelter. If Victor turned his attention away for a few seconds, he might have a chance of grabbing it.

Jake checked Victor's position, his heart skipping a beat as he realized their pursuer had moved several feet closer, the distance between them only a few yards now.

Suddenly, Mariah's hand closed around his wrist, her fingers digging in. He found her gazing up at the tiny pieces of twilight sky peeking through the pine needles above them. "Do you hear that?" she mouthed.

A second later, he heard the sound of a helicopter approaching, its rotor blades beating an unmistakable cadence.

Jake shot a quick look at Victor. The older man heard the rhythmic *thump-thump* of the helicopter's rotor blades as well, craning his neck for a better view of the approaching aircraft. Suddenly, he reversed course and began running at breakneck speed, legs churning, back in the direction of his house.

Mariah dropped her head to her hands, her breath coming in soft, rapid gasps. "Too close," she breathed.

Jake wrapped his arms around her, sharing in a moment of relief. He breathed in the scent of her damp hair, still fragrant with remnants of the apple-scented shampoo he'd come to associate with her. For a second, his heart seemed to squeeze into a tight ball.

"We should get out of here." She nestled more firmly into his embrace. "Maybe we could wave down the helicopter—"

"They won't see us through the trees."

"You called Gabe before we left the motel. Maybe he's wondering why we haven't called in yet. He could have called the local police—"

"It's too early," he disagreed. "We weren't expected

back in Gossamer Ridge yet, and it's not unusual for cell phone coverage to be spotty on the road. They won't send out an alarm before late tonight, and even then, they'll start looking for interstate accidents first."

He knew, if they lasted long enough out here, his family would descend on the area in an avenging horde. But not yet.

And the key part, anyway, was lasting long enough for the cavalry to arrive.

"I think we're safer staying put," he decided.

Sighing, she leaned back against him, her curvy backside pressed flush between his thighs. All thoughts of comfort fled, his whole body going hot and hard with unexpected need.

He struggled with the urge to slide his hands up her body to cup her breasts. The timing was terrible, their situation even worse, and that was before he even took her injury into consideration. Yet, in the middle of this mess her secrets had wrought, he still wanted Mariah.

Lies, danger and all.

"He'll come back and find us," she protested. "The helicopter will go away and he'll come out to hunt."

"Why did he run away in the first place?"

Mariah released a little huff of mirthless laughter. "Ever been the target of a manhunt?"

"Can't say I have."

"Well, Victor has."

KARL HAD TURNED HIM IN. Maybe he'd been caught dumping the truck. Or someone had seen Victor forcing Marisol and her husband into the van. Or maybe his fugitives had found their way out of the woods to the main highway seven miles down the road. They'd have had time to walk there by now, assuming they lucked into the right direction.

Victor locked his front door and pressed his ear to the wood, listening to the beat of the helicopter's blades overhead. The sound lingered, as if the craft were circling the woods, looking for a clearing large enough for a safe landing. He checked the Taurus. Seven shells in the cylinder. He might not make it out alive, but he could take a few bastards with him.

A trilling sound nearby made him jump like a skittish rabbit. It took a couple of seconds to realize it was a cell phone ringing.

His cell phone was in his pocket, silent. It had to be coming from the stuff he'd taken from Marisol's truck.

He followed the sound until he found a phone tucked into the pocket of the larger of the two suitcases. On the glowing display, he saw a name. Gabe Cooper.

Answering the call was out of the question, of course. But even after the ringing stopped, the phantom trill remained in his head, filling it until even the *whump-whump* of the helicopter rotor blades faded into silence.

It took a few minutes to realize he wasn't hearing the helicopter because it had left the sky overhead.

Had it landed? Or had it moved on?

Victor dragged a chair from the kitchen table to the front door, settling a few feet behind the solid wood, the Taurus in his lap. If the helicopter had landed on the road and there were cops headed his way, he'd know about it soon enough.

And if there weren't?

As soon as the sun came up, he'd go hunting again.

"AT FIRST, I DIDN'T REMEMBER anything but the screaming." Mariah had scooted away from Jake, her body in profile, as soon as she started telling him about the hit-and-run. The pain in her voice was palpable. Clearly, she had never moved past the tragedy of losing Micah's father, only hidden it beneath a facade of half truths and full-blown lies.

It explained so much, really. Her constant reserve. Her occasional nightmares and the deep sense of sadness that permeated every moment of their life, even the happy ones.

He wanted to touch her, driven this time not by lust but by a human need to offer comfort to someone so obviously in pain. But her hunched, hands-off posture was too obvious to ignore. He kept his hands to himself.

"Who was screaming?" he asked.

"I was." She shuddered, hugging herself more tightly. "I still don't remember what Micah's body looked like, even though I was holding him there in the street. I mean, I saw pictures at the trial, but I don't remember the actual moment."

"Maybe it's better that way."

She slanted a look at him. He could barely see her in the deepening darkness. They didn't dare start a fire for heat and illumination, of course, but the clouds above broke now and then to reveal the pale face of the rising moon. It was visible now through the pine boughs over their head, filtering through the needles to bathe their shelter with milky-blue moon glow. The pale effulgence outlined her profile and made her gray eyes glow like molten silver.

"I didn't remember the moment of impact, either. Not then."

"So you didn't realize it was Victor?"

"The police said I was in shock. They wanted to take me to the hospital, but I was afraid to go."

"Why?"

"I don't know. I just needed to go home."

"To Victor's?" He slanted a look of surprise her way. Had her life before been so horrible that she had seen a man like Victor as a preferable alternative?

She managed a bleak smile. "You have to understand. Victor was like a father to me. He took me in when I was lost. He educated me. Taught me to read for comprehension and insight, to learn things just for the joy of it. He showed me a world I never thought I could be part of."

"He was like a mentor?" Jake asked, trying to understand. He had trouble picturing the man who'd just taken them at gunpoint as some sort of intellectual.

"Don't underestimate him," she warned. "He's smarter than people think."

"Was it—sexual? Between you and Victor?"

She blanched. "God, no. Never like that. He really was sort of like a father. Or, at least, what I thought a father might be like. I knew he didn't like Micah, that it angered him when I talked about him. But I thought it was concern for me. I couldn't conceive that he'd ever do what he did."

"But you wanted to go back home after what you witnessed?"

"I told you, I didn't really remember what happened at that point. I just wanted to go home to someone I thought cared about me." She pressed her forehead against her knees, bunched into a ball of misery. "I should have known it was too good to be true. The good things that happen to me always are."

Like me? Jake wondered. Or had she ever seen him as anything but a buffer between her and Victor's wrath?

She looked up at him suddenly, as if she realized what she'd just admitted. "I didn't mean you—"

"What happened when you got home?" he asked, not yet

ready for a deeper analysis of their sham of a relationship. His doubts were already on the verge of overwhelming him at a time when he needed his focus intact.

"Victor was there. He was acting strangely, until he realized I didn't remember seeing him."

"I thought you said he wanted you to know it was him."

"He did. He was—disappointed. You see, he'd already put a plan in place, and my temporary memory loss threw things in flux. Victor doesn't like to have his plans thwarted."

"Yeah, I get that feeling," Jake murmured.

"He wanted me to know. He was already planning to torment me, and he wasn't going to be stopped." Her voice dropped an octave, shaking.

"What did he do?" Jake wasn't sure he really wanted to know, but he sensed she needed to tell him.

"He showed me the car. The smashed headlights. The dents in the bumper." Her voice caught, and she had to clear her throat to add, "The blood."

"My God."

"It came back to me, seeing the evidence. I remembered it all. The look on his face as he got Micah in his sights— he was smiling. Not laughing. Not mad. Just a simple smile of accomplishment." Mariah lifted one hand to scrape back her tangled hair, wincing as the movement stretched her undershirt against her side. Her hand dropped quickly to cover the bandanna he'd put there earlier. "I think I'm bleeding again."

Jake scooted closer and plucked her shirt away from the bandage. The back of his hand brushed against the side of her breast and she sucked in a quick breath.

Her eyes locked with his, and he felt his bones begin to

liquefy. Swallowing the hot lump in his throat, he rasped, "Did I hurt you?"

She shook her head, her lips trembling apart.

He forced his mind to the task of checking her wound, knowing that giving in to the need for closeness would complicate everything—and solve nothing. He dared a quick flick of the butane lighter for a better look at the wound. All thoughts of sex fled his mind at the sight of the swollen, inflamed skin around the ragged edges of the bullet graze.

The wound was already becoming infected.

"Is it bad?" Mariah asked.

He couldn't afford to sugarcoat the truth. There'd been enough deceit between them as it was. "I think you've got some infection setting in."

She released a quiet huff of breath. "How bad?"

"Just starting, but we'll need to keep an eye on it."

"We need the first-aid kit from the truck."

"We can try to find a way out of here first thing in the morning," he promised, tying the bandanna back in place. "But we're up against enough of a disadvantage even without the darkness to contend with." And if Victor was at all smart, he'd have already moved the truck off the road where it would be harder to find, Jake added silently.

"I saw a first-aid kit back at Victor's." She pressed her hand against the homemade bandage. "Too bad I didn't think to stick a tube of antibiotic in my pocket before we left."

"We were a little busy."

She managed a tiny smile. "And at the time, I didn't know I'd need it."

"You were lucky. He could have been a better shot."

She resumed her tucked position, resting her chin on the valley between her bent knees. She had shifted positions so that this time, she sat facing him, her eyes shining in the dim moonlight. "I couldn't let him kill you, too."

His heart squeezed, even though he was pretty sure even this small show of concern for him was somehow wrapped up in losing Micah Davis three years ago. He'd known from the moment he met her there would always be a part of her that belonged to another man. He'd thought he could live with the knowledge.

Now he wasn't so sure.

"You should try to get some sleep," he suggested.

"No. I slept earlier. You should sleep."

"I'm not the one with the bullet wound." He scooted back to give her room to stretch out on the ground.

She looked as if she were going to argue, but she finally gave in and lay on her good side, her hand still pressing lightly against her injury. It must be hurting her a little, he thought, joining her in wishing they'd had a chance to steal some first-aid supplies.

"He locked me in the basement for two days," she said quietly, breaking the tense silence beginning to rise between them in the stifled confines of the shelter. "And removed the bulb from the only light fixture."

Jake's heart turned a sympathetic flip. One thing he was certain of, even now, was her fear of dark, confined places. He'd seen her panic firsthand one time she was accidentally locked in a storeroom at the bait shop his parents ran back in Gossamer Ridge. "You must have been terrified."

She looked at him, her eyes narrowed slightly, as if she were trying to gauge his sincerity. "I thought I was going to die there. Maybe I would have if another witness hadn't come forward and put the cops on Victor's trail."

"The cops found you?"

"Yeah." She looked away from him, her eyelids drooping. "That's when they went after him. They caught up with him the next day, after a countywide manhunt."

He wanted to ask her for more details, but her eyes had already drifted shut. Within a few minutes, she was asleep, her body relaxed and her breathing slow and even.

Keeping his ears open for any unusual sounds outside their shelter, Jake watched his wife sleep, his heart as heavy as stone in his chest, interfering with his own respiration.

How could he have not known she was lying to him all this time? Not just a little fib, either; she'd told fundamental lies about who she was.

"Marisol Mendez." He spoke the name aloud, too softly to disturb his sleeping wife, just to see how it felt as it rolled over his tongue.

Strange. It felt strange.

She'd told Victor that Mariah Davis Cooper really was her name, that she'd had it changed legally. Hell, maybe she had. But how could Jake know for sure, short of tracking down the court records himself?

He used to believe everything she told him. How many of her statements had been nothing but bald-faced lies?

She'd told him she'd grown up in Texas, which appeared to be the truth. But she'd also told him her parents were dead, and now it turned out that she'd never known her father and her mother was a crack addict she probably hadn't seen in years.

She'd told him Micah's father had been her late husband. Now he knew she'd never been married to Micah's father at all, because the psychotic Pygmalion she was living with had run Micah Davis down with his car.

Of course, that was assuming that part was true. Right now, he wasn't sure what was true and what was just another one of Mariah's fabrications.

What was real about their relationship? Was anything?

She'd told Jake she loved him. Was that also a lie?

And what about what he'd told her? Did he love her? Had he ever?

Could he ever?

God, he had to get out of this cramped little hiding hole. Just for a minute. He needed air.

He took care emerging from the cocoon of the pine-bough shelter, standing up straight only after he'd scanned the area in all directions for any sign of human habitation. Breathing deeply, he filled his lungs with cool, rain-washed air. The world around him smelled earthy and primal.

The downpour had stopped for now, though the sky overhead was starting to darken with thick, moisture-laden clouds again. It would probably be raining again in the morning, but for now, there were enough clear-sky breaks in the clouds to afford him intermittent moonlight to light his path.

He checked his watch. It was later than he realized— nearly 10:00 p.m. He'd seen and heard no sign of anyone searching the area since Victor had run away from the helicopter.

He ventured farther north, away from Victor's place, to see if he could gauge how far the woods went before they ran into another clearing or some other break in the trees. He was afraid to go too far, afraid Victor might start hunting for them again without notice. He couldn't afford to drop his guard for even a minute.

He'd gone little more than half a mile when he started to hear the sound of rushing water. The noise grew in intensity as he moved farther north, until it drowned out the natural sounds of birds and night creatures prowling the woods.

He reached the edge of the woods, where they dropped off precipitously down a steep embankment to a creek below. In normal conditions, he supposed the creek was no more than ten feet across and probably shallow enough to ford with little effort. Now, however, after two days of driving rain, the creek was swollen well beyond its banks, muddy and tumultuous as it raced west where it must eventually flow into the Leaf River.

Even if they could figure a way to cross the creek, there was nothing on the other side but trees and underbrush, as far as Jake could see.

There might be a break in the woods if they angled either east or west, but it might be miles away. Meanwhile, he knew there was a road to the south, one that would take them past Victor's house and eventually back to the bigger road where their truck had broken down.

The best way home would be to go back the way they'd come.

Disheartened, he made his way back to the shelter, where he found Mariah still asleep. If nothing else, he noted with faint gratitude, his trek to the creek had managed to shift his mood.

He lay next to her, lending her his body heat as he'd promised, and forced himself to think only one breath to the next, not what might happen days and weeks from now. He wasn't happy that she'd lied to him. He wasn't sure if their marriage could survive when it was built on a foundation of deception. Hers or his.

But she was an injured woman in need of medical aid, and there was a ruthless, deadly man standing between them and safety. She wasn't lying about that, at the very least.

Questions about their marriage could wait.

First, they had to make it through this mess alive.

Chapter Eight

Warm hands moved over her face, the palms a little rough and wonderfully familiar. Mariah turned her face toward the heat of Jake's touch, a faint sense of anxiety nibbling at the edges of her sense of well-being. But Jake's body lay warm and firm against hers, and his strong, gentle fingers traced lightly along the curve of her jaw, and she couldn't imagine how anything could possibly be wrong about waking up in his arms.

Until she tried to move.

Agony exploded in her side, pain ripping through her nervous system like shrapnel. She snapped open her eyes and froze in place, afraid to move again.

"No sudden moves." Jake eased her into a better position.

Memory flooded her numb brain as she registered the cold, the dampness, the spiky pine needle walls surrounding them. They were still in the cramped, dark hovel of a shelter Jake had fashioned from broken pine boughs. A six-inch gouge marred her side where a bullet meant for Jake had grazed her instead.

And then the memory of their encounter with Victor Logan, the malevolent ghost of her inescapable past, flooded back. He was still out there somewhere, hunting for them.

"You're running a fever." Jake withdrew his hands from her face and peered at the faintly lit dial of his watch. Gray light seeped through the tiny gaps in the pine branches overhead, signifying morning. At least it hadn't rained all night. Some of her clothing had almost dried while she slept.

Moving gingerly into a sitting position, she bit her lip as new bursts of pain detonated in the ravaged skin of her side.

"Let me take a look." Jake started to pull up her bloody shirt but stopped, his blue eyes seeking hers for permission.

Mariah's heart sank. Two days ago, he wouldn't have felt the need to ask whether or not he could touch her. "Go ahead," she said, her voice ragged with pain. But she blinked back her burning tears. She'd made the mistakes. She'd damned well pay for them without whining or sending Jake on a guilt trip just because he was hurt and angry about her deception.

She was getting exactly what she deserved.

Jake checked under the bandage, wincing in sympathy as the bandanna stuck to dried blood on her skin, eliciting a quick gasp of pain from her dry throat. "Sorry!"

"It's okay," she said through clenched teeth. "How does it look this morning?"

"Not really much different than last night," he answered, although she could tell from the deepening furrows on his forehead that he wasn't telling her the whole truth.

She arched her neck to get a look at the wound herself. The gouge was something out of a nightmare, ragged and oozing blood and serous fluid. Even in the low light, she could see how red and swollen the skin around the wound had become.

"It's infected," she said flatly, trying not to panic.

"That's not unexpected," Jake murmured, sitting back on his heels. "Why don't we let it air out a little?"

"We don't have time," she said, more annoyed than reassured by his unflappable calm. "We've got a crazy man out there looking for us, and God knows who took a potshot at him and why." Her head began to swim, whether from distress or from the blood she'd lost. She was probably already dehydrated. "We need food and water. First-aid supplies."

"I know."

"We can't hole up here the rest of the day." She put her hand to her forehead, fighting off the odd sense of imbalance. "I need water. I've lost too much blood."

"There's a creek north of here, but it's muddy and swollen. I should have thought to put out a container to collect water." He sounded annoyed for not thinking of it sooner.

"How do you know there's a creek north of here?"

"I did a little scouting last night while you were asleep."

Her heart turned a flip. "Alone? With Victor out there looking for us?"

"I kept an eye out."

She felt a bubble of hysteria rising in her throat and struggled to keep it from emerging. "You just wanted to get away from me, right?"

"That had nothing to do with it."

"But you do want to get away from me." She clamped her fingers together, her bones rattling on the inside as if the earth around her were shaking. She clenched her teeth to keep them from chattering. "I don't blame you. I know you must feel so betrayed. I would in your position."

"Then why didn't you just tell me the truth from the beginning?" he asked bluntly.

She lost her grip on the shudders racking her body. A series of violent chills flowed through her, until her whole body was knotted with the shakes.

Jake scooted closer, taking her face between his big, strong hands. His expression darkened. "Your fever is worse."

"I don't get the chills unless it's a high one," she said, the words stuttering through her clacking teeth.

He tugged at the collar of her sweater. "Let's let nature do the work of getting your temperature down."

After laying her sweater to the side, he stripped off his own undershirt, put his sweater back on and stepped outside the shelter for a few seconds. When he returned, the undershirt was wet. Lifting her mane of hair out of the way, he laid the wet compress against the back of her neck. The cold sensation sent a shock wave rippling through her body, and she bit back a gasp.

"Hold this in place for a few minutes. I'll be back before you know it." He slipped out of the shelter again before she could say another word.

Mariah gingerly scooted closer to the inner perimeter of the shelter, trying to peer between tree branches to see if she could spot Jake. But he was already out of sight.

She settled back, trying to find a position that didn't hurt like hell, and focused on trying to relax her tense, aching muscles. All the stress wasn't exactly helping her fight off the infection ravaging her side.

By the time Jake had been gone for several minutes, Mariah began to worry. Even with an emotional chasm between them as wide as the Mississippi River, she still felt the connection, the indefinable pull that had brought them together in the first place.

Was it love? It wasn't the same emotion she'd felt with Micah, but she wasn't sure she ever wanted to feel that much love for anyone again. She'd always fancied herself a survivor, able to deal with whatever blows the merciless world flung her way. But losing Micah had damned near killed her.

Maybe it had been the pain of having him ripped away when she finally thought she'd climbed over the last major hurdle of her life and was finally going to be happy and free.

She should have known better.

If she hadn't had Victor's trial and her surprise pregnancy to keep her putting one foot in front of the other during that horrible time, she wasn't sure she'd have lived through those bleak days following Micah's murder. Having her baby to love—and Victor to hate—had kept her going.

She didn't know how people survived losing someone they loved to murder when there was no justice or hope to be had. The constant push-pull of hope and despair would have destroyed her long before now. At least she knew who'd killed Micah.

What about people like Jake's brother J.D.? Over a decade had passed since his wife's unsolved murder, and somehow, he soldiered on. Having family around to support him must help, of course. And he'd had his two kids to take care of.

Still, J.D. was haunted by her murder. The very first day Mariah had walked into the Cooper Cove Marina bait shop, she'd stepped into the middle of a family crisis because a hot lead into the murder had turned out to be a complete bust.

She could still remember the look in J. D. Cooper's eyes when he realized he was as far away from finding his wife's killer as he'd ever been. *Tortured* wasn't too strong a word to describe the way he'd looked at that moment.

That's why she hadn't told them her real reason for coming to Chickasaw County, Alabama, in the first place. A lie of omission, perhaps, but still a lie.

But why hadn't she told Jake the truth about the rest of her secrets? He wasn't the kind of guy who'd have held her past against her if she'd just told him everything.

What was it, really, that had driven her to silence?

Fear that, like Victor, he wasn't the man he seemed to be? Or the growing certainty that Jake was keeping secrets, too?

FROM JAKE'S HIDDEN vantage point in the woods edging Victor Logan's property, the house looked dark and quiet. Victor could be asleep. Or he could be out in the woods, looking for them.

Either way, Jake needed to be quick and quiet. He knew Victor was still armed.

The temptation to break into the house was strong. Mariah had seen a first-aid kit inside, bound to be full of bandages, ointments and fever reducers. And they could both use a little food; it had been hours since they'd eaten anything.

But water was the most important thing. Blood loss and fever would speed up dehydration, and dehydration along with the blood loss was probably messing with her blood pressure already, if her earlier lightheadedness was anything to go by.

He had to get fluids in her. Now. And his best choice for an acceptably clean water supply was the outdoor faucet Jake had spotted a few seconds earlier, just as he hoped he would.

Now he just had to figure out a way to find a container and get the water without Victor discovering him.

A corner angle of attack was the smartest choice. Even

if Victor was awake, looking out his windows, the corner created a large blind spot. If Jake could reach the side of the house unseen, he could move about freely below the window line.

He couldn't wait much longer. The eastern sky was quickly turning from silky gray to faint rose. Though the last weather forecast he'd heard promised more rain was on the way, there might be a few hours of daylight before the sky blackened again.

Daylight was not his friend.

A light came on in one of the two visible windows. Jake's heart jumped into his throat, and he stepped back into the deeper cover behind a Japanese honeysuckle vine. The pale yellow flowers were heavy with nectar, filling the air around him with a heady, sweet scent that reminded him of roaming the woods of Gossamer Ridge as a boy.

He would give almost anything to be back there now, surrounded by his family. His mother would have good advice about how to handle his crushing sense of betrayal. His brother Gabe would have his back, whatever he chose to do.

Better yet, he'd like to have his brothers with him right here, right now, surrounding Victor's cabin the way they'd surrounded the guest cabin up on Gossamer Ridge last November when his brother Luke returned home after ten years away with a gang of South American narco-terrorists and a deadly unit of corrupt and ruthless mercenaries on his heels. Even armed to the teeth and holding hostages, neither group had been a match for seven armed Coopers who knew the woods and hills of Gossamer Ridge as well as anyone in the world.

Pushing aside his futile wishes, he watched as the light went off. A faint glow coming from around the far corner of the house suggested another light had come on, this time in one of the front rooms, in an area not visible from Jake's position.

And if he couldn't see Victor, Victor couldn't see him.

Slipping from the cover of the honeysuckle vine, Jake darted across the narrow strip of winter-brown lawn and pressed himself flat against the weathered clapboard. The wood was waterlogged from the two days of rain, long overdue for weatherproofing. Jake supposed Victor had more pressing concerns than routine upkeep on his house.

Like seeking revenge on the woman who'd put him in jail.

Carefully, he moved closer to the nearest window. If he stood upright, he could just see over the bottom sash of the window. He darted a quick look inside, seeing a neat, sparsely furnished bedroom. This was the window where he'd seen the light earlier, so he guessed it must be Victor's bedroom. It was dark now, but he could see light coming from the hallway just beyond the open bedroom door.

Jake ducked out of sight quickly as a silhouette moved across the doorway. His heart pounding wildly, he almost missed the sound of water running. It took a couple of seconds to realize the rushing sound in his ears wasn't his racing pulse.

Victor must be taking a shower. Perfect. The sound of the shower would stifle any noise from the outdoor spigot.

Jake made a quick half circuit of the house until he spotted a watering can sitting at the edge of the front porch. It lay on its side, probably not used in some time. It was plastic, rather than metal, which meant rust hadn't built up, though a thin layer of muddy grime coated the faded red plastic exterior.

Jake reached around the side of the house, exposing

himself as little as possible, and grabbed the plastic container. Hurrying back to the spigot, he gave the ancient-looking wheel-shaped knob a strong twist. The handle made a high-pitched squeak as bits of rust gave way, sending Jake's already speeding heart into the stratosphere, but water finally poured from the faucet, rusty at first but soon going clear.

Jake decided he had to take time to at least rinse the dirt from the watering can before filling it, but the action ate up precious seconds he wasn't sure he had. With the outdoor faucet running, it was hard to tell if the shower inside was still going. As he filled the container, he mentally calculated how long it would take for Victor to shower and sent up a quick prayer that their former captor was the extra-clean type.

Finally, the can was filled about two-thirds of the way to the top. It would make for a heavy burden on the trip back to Mariah, but Jake could handle it.

He turned off the water, panicking for a moment when he realized he no longer heard the sound of the shower. Tucking the water container close to keep it from sloshing around, he pressed his back against the side of the house and listened for sounds within.

Light poured from the nearest window, the room Jake had decided must be Victor's bedroom. He froze in place, trying to hear through any sound of movement within. Faintly, he heard the sound of whistling—a classical tune he recognized, though he couldn't have come up with the name if asked.

Mariah had warned him not to underestimate Victor, Jake remembered. He wasn't stupid.

But he was a bundle of raw nerves. Jake had seen that much in his eyes the day before when everything had started going to hell. Mariah had also said Victor hated for his plans to go awry. So, a control freak.

He'd probably notice the missing watering can. Jake would have to make sure he was as far from this place as possible when that happened.

The sound of whistling faded. Jake dared a quick look through the window and saw Victor heading toward the front of the house.

Jake took a chance and darted across the yard and into the woods, stopping when he was safely hidden by the same clump of honeysuckle he'd used for cover earlier. He heard the creak of a door opening and the sounds of footsteps on the front porch. Staying in a crouch, Jake moved laterally until he had a decent view of the front yard.

The van was still parked in front of the house, though Victor had switched out the front tire for the spare. Jake spotted Victor disappearing through the van's side door.

Victor must have changed the tire sometime during the previous afternoon. But why? Had he needed to drive somewhere?

The truck, Jake realized with dismay. Victor had gone to move the truck and the boat. He couldn't afford for the vehicle to stay on the road long. Sooner or later, someone might call it in as abandoned and the cops would want to know why.

What have you done with my boat, Victor?

A soft buzzing sound drifted toward Jake's hiding place, and he could barely make out Victor moving around inside the van's cargo area. After a few minutes the buzzing sound ceased, and Victor emerged from the belly of the van, carrying a small hand-held electric vacuum cleaner. Removing any evidence that Jake and Mariah had ever stepped foot in the van?

Of course, for that little bit of subterfuge to work, he'd

have to dispose of the vacuum cleaner somewhere, Jake thought as he watched Victor go back into the house. Victor would also have to dispose of his clothes from yesterday. And he'd have had to vacuum the living room and the basement as well to remove any trace evidence that he and Mariah had been down there.

As if Jake had given him a cue, Victor emerged from the house again carrying a large black plastic garbage bag. He tossed the closed container into the van's cargo area.

He was leaving, Jake realized. Which would give him time to take a look around the house.

Suddenly, a soft crackling sound behind him made Jake's hair stand on end. He swiveled his head and spotted Mariah creeping toward him. She was pale beneath her olive skin, dark circles smudging the skin under her big gray eyes. She was looking toward the van, clearly aware of Victor's presence.

To her credit, she was crouched as low as he was, staying out of sight. But that fact didn't make Jake's galloping heart slow down even a notch.

The van cranked to life, the sound jangling Jake's taut nerves. Mariah scooted closer, sliding in behind him where he peered through the green leaves of a forsythia bush. Most of the yellow blooms were gone by now, but the leaves gave them plenty of cover. At least, Jake hoped so.

Victor backed the van out, swinging around in a lazy circle until the cab was heading forward down the dirt road. Mariah took a deep breath as if to speak, but Jake whispered a quick "shh" and she fell silent.

Only after the van was completely out of sight did he turn to look at her. "What the hell are you doing here?"

"Looking for you," she answered, wobbling a little. He caught her before she fell back on her butt.

"You're weak as a kitten. You shouldn't be traipsing around the woods after me," he growled, helping her to her feet.

She swayed toward him. "I don't traipse."

He pushed aside his frustration and looked back at the now-empty house. This might be their best chance to grab the first-aid supplies they needed. But what if Victor came back while they were inside?

"What are you doing here?" she countered.

He motioned to the water container sitting on the ground beside him. "You said you were dehydrated."

She looked down at the water, almost licking her lips in anticipation. But she forced her attention up again, gazing toward the muddy road down which the van had disappeared. "Where is Victor going?"

"He had a garbage bag. Earlier he vacuumed out the van."

"Getting rid of evidence?"

"I think so," he answered.

"He could dump it anywhere in the woods around here. It might not be found for years."

"Maybe," Jake conceded. "But he'd want it as far from these particular woods as possible."

"So at least a few miles. That gives us time to get inside and out again before he comes back." Mariah started walking unsteadily toward the house.

Jake caught her wrist, stopping her. "I'm not sure—"

"My fever's going up." She wrapped her arms around herself, and he saw that she was shaking again. "At the very least, I need something like ibuprofen to bring it down."

And if they could find some sort of antiseptic in the first-aid kit, he could give the wound a decent cleaning and bandage her up properly. They might get lucky and stop the infection before it got any worse.

"Okay," he conceded. "But you'll stay at the window and keep watch."

She gave him an odd look.

"What?" he asked when she didn't speak.

"I think there's something else we should look for, while we're in there," she said softly, her eyes warm with sympathy.

His brow furrowed. "Like what?"

"There's another thing I haven't told you about why I showed up in Gossamer Ridge three years ago," she said softly, reluctance written on her face.

More secrets? His stomach knotted. "What is it?"

"When I was locked up in the basement at Victor's, I found something. A binder. A scrapbook, really." Mariah pushed her tangled hair away from her face, looking away. "It was a bunch of newspaper clippings about some murders."

The knot in Jake's stomach tightened. "Murders?"

"Murdered women. I didn't get to take it with me when I escaped, and the police never found it later. By the time Victor finished smearing me, they pretty much believed I had made it up to make sure he got the book thrown at him for Micah's murder, but I know what I saw." She looked up, meeting his gaze squarely. "Jake, one of the newspaper clippings was from the *Chickasaw County Herald*."

Don't say it, Jake thought, a toxic blend of hope and fear burning the back of his eyes.

"It was about your sister-in-law," Mariah said. Her expression grew even more pained, as if she had to force the words from her mouth. She put her hand on his arm, the display of compassion scaring him more than the thoughts running through his head. He dreaded the next words he saw trembling on her lips.

She took a deep breath and spoke what he suspected

was the final piece of truth she'd withheld from him all this time. "Jake, I think Victor knows something about Brenda's murder. I think he could even be involved."

Chapter Nine

Jake looked as if she'd punched him in the gut. "Brenda's murder? Victor?"

Mariah's heart ached at what she saw in his eyes. There was disbelief, but there was also a faint light of hope. Jake hadn't been as affected by his sister-in-law's death as his brother J.D., of course, or even his twin, Gabe, who blamed himself for a foolish mistake that had kept him from reaching Brenda in time to stop her killer. But the Cooper family was close-knit and protective of each other.

What hurt one of them hurt them all.

Jake had suffered through all the red herrings and false leads of Brenda's cold case as much as any of the Coopers. He'd seen leads grow hot and cold, saw the way every dashed hope had sliced away a piece of his brother J.D.'s soul.

The family needed closure, and Jake would listen to her theory because he had no other choice. He wanted to believe her, even as he dreaded it.

If she was wrong about Victor this time, he'd be crushed.

But she'd lied enough. This was the last secret she'd been keeping. She had to let him make his own decision about whether or not he believed it could be true.

"I'm not a hundred percent sure I'm right," she admitted.

But even as she expressed uncertainty aloud, she realized she really didn't have many doubts about her theory now. Victor had already proved he had the capacity for murder, twice over. And if he'd been living in Chickasaw County at the time, he might have had dealings with the trucking company Brenda had worked with, since he was an auto mechanic by trade.

Maybe Brenda had said something to him in the course of idle conversation, something perfectly innocent on her part, that he'd taken as a slight. A man like Victor Logan wouldn't respond well to perceived insults, especially from a woman he would have seen as his intellectual inferior. "He used to move from town to town in his younger days. He could have been in Chickasaw County at the time of her death—"

Jake stared at her as if seeing her for the first time. "Why the hell didn't you tell us?"

She looked away, feeling the full brunt of his hurt. "You remember the day I showed up," she said, her voice a soft rasp. "J.D. had just had that lead from Scottsboro fall through—"

"He was crushed," Jake said tightly. "You saw what not knowing was doing to him. What it's still doing to him. How could you keep quiet all this time?"

"I didn't know if you'd believe me," she answered, aware of how inadequate the excuse sounded. "I didn't know if I was even right about the theory. I still don't. Victor's a true crime buff—maybe he was just keeping track of the murders for his own research. He might have had nothing to do with it—"

"You found the scrapbook four years ago. Four years, Mariah. You sat on this for four years."

"I'm sorry," she whispered.

His lips pressed into a tight line, as if he were struggling to keep his anger in check. After a deep breath, he looked at her again. "Think he still has the scrapbook?"

"I don't know," she admitted. "Maybe. I did a little reading in his true crime library, too. If he had any part in what happened to Brenda or those other women in that binder, he was probably holding on to the clippings like trophies. He wouldn't have gotten rid of it permanently."

Jake looked at the house, his brow furrowed. Every emotion he was feeling was evident on his face, open to her in a way his heart no longer was. He wanted to go inside and look around almost as much as he wanted to take his next breath.

He also dreaded what he'd find.

"If you don't want to go in there—" she started.

"No. We need the first-aid kit, if nothing else." Jake started walking toward the house, not waiting for her.

She followed, not able to keep up with his purposeful stride. He slowed at the porch steps, waiting for her. She was already out of breath, hard pain burning her wounded side.

"Sorry." He helped her ascend the porch steps. "Don't suppose you know where he'd stash a spare key?"

She looked around the porch, trying to spot a likely place. Victor was wily, but he was also a creature of almost obsessive habit. At the other house in Buckley, he'd kept the spare key on a homemade set of wind chimes made of old keys hanging on fishing wire. There were no wind chimes here, but he'd probably try to hide the key in plain sight the same way.

The porch was mostly bare, save for a rickety pine rocking chair that had probably come with the house when he moved in, and a terra-cotta pot filled with dying winter pansies. The flower pot was too obvious. The rocker was a possibility, though. She crouched by the chair, trying not to topple over as her head began to swim wildly.

Jake hunkered down behind her, his chest solid and warm against her back, holding her up. She ran her fingers under the chair seat, the rough cane bottom scratchy on her fingers. Near the back, she felt a bulge in the strip of cane. Examining the bulge, she found an opening in the weave and pushed one finger inside, praying she hadn't discovered a sleeping lizard or a beetle's lair. Her finger touched something cold and hard.

Tugging, she extracted a thin brass key and held it up for Jake to see. "I guess this is it."

Swallowing the questions she could see he wanted to ask, he tried the key in the lock. The door swung open with a creak that made the hair on Mariah's neck rise to attention.

He didn't turn on any lights. Probably a good idea, since they didn't know where Victor was going or how long he'd be gone. No need to give him a reason to put his guard up.

"Stay here by the window," Jake told her. "There's a long view down the road so you'll see him coming in plenty of time."

Let's pray it doesn't come to that, she thought.

"Where did you see the first-aid kit?" he asked.

"On a shelf in the basement." She leaned her hot face against the cool pane of glass, keeping her eyes on the muddy road winding through the woods south of the house. Gunmetal-colored clouds scudded across the sky, moving east, bringing in the promised rain. The first fat splats of rain hit the mud puddles dotting Victor's drab front yard.

"What about the scrapbook? What am I looking for?"

She turned away from the window to meet his gaze.

"Last time I saw it, it was in a black binder. I don't know if it's still in the same one. It's been four years."

"It'll still be a binder. We'll find it."

Mariah's gut recoiled at the thought. Seeing the binder all those years ago had opened her eyes to how much she'd deceived herself where Victor was concerned. Despite warning Jake earlier that the binder might be nothing more than an extension of his interest in true crime stories, she'd known better, even four years ago.

She knew he was somehow involved with those murders.

THE BASEMENT WAS DARK and musty. It had also been recently cleaned, the floor spotless where it had been slightly grimy the day before when Victor brought them down here.

Jake scanned the shelves for the first-aid kit first, knowing it was the priority. Even in the hour since he'd left her at the shelter, she'd deteriorated, her face gray beneath her natural tan and her eyes sunken and glazed with fever. He couldn't afford to waste any time down here.

He found the first-aid kit on the shelf, just as she'd said. The soft-bodied container was made of bright blue nylon, full of bandages, ointments and over-the-counter medications in individual tear-open packets tucked in pockets inside the zippered pouch. His truck kit was bigger and more extensive, but this one would have to do.

"Jake!" Mariah's cry from upstairs set Jake's hair on end. Shoving the first-aid pouch into the waistband of his trousers as he ran, he bounded up the cellar steps and burst into the living room, not even thinking about stealth. If Victor was back—or the second shooter had made another appearance—

But the living room was empty except for Mariah, who was holding up a pair of women's jeans.

"These are mine," she said softly. Next to her on the floor was a large cardboard box labeled Goodwill. The top was open, revealing a neatly folded stack of clothing.

Jake spotted the warm cable-knit sweater he liked to wear when fishing during colder weather. The box was filled with the clothes that had been inside their suitcases, although the suitcases were nowhere to be found.

Mariah was already gathering up dry clothes, her eyes alight. "They're so warm," she breathed, her voice trembling.

He checked out the front window quickly to make sure the area was clear. By the time he looked back at Mariah, she was already stripping off her damp, bloodstained undershirt.

"Careful," he said as the hem caught on the edge of the bandanna covering her bullet graze, eliciting a soft cry of pain from her pale lips. He caught her hands. "It's too dangerous to try to do this here. Victor's removing evidence—maybe he just forgot this box and will double back to get it."

Her expression fell. He felt guilty about dashing her hopes for clean, dry clothes.

"Tell you what," he conceded. "We'll switch out our wet clothes for a dry set and put our dirty clothes in there, at the bottom in case he checks. Deal?"

The grin that split her face was nearly blinding in intensity. She removed her shirt and grabbed a teal-blue sweater lying folded on the top of the stack.

"Not the sweater," Jake warned. "Rain's coming, and a wet sweater will get soggy and weigh you down. Plus, it's not much in the way of camouflage. Wear this instead." He handed her a flannel shirt in a dark-green plaid.

She also snatched clean underwear from the pile. "I wish we had time for a shower."

"So do I," he admitted. He felt as if he'd spent the last twenty-four hours wallowing in mud.

"At least a quick sponge off?" she suggested hopefully.

He weighed the dangers. There was still no sign of Victor's van down the road. If she was quick—

"Okay. But let's make it quick. You first. Try not to make a mess—we need to clean up behind us if we can so he won't know we were here."

As she headed for the bathroom, she flashed him a bright grin that lit up her pale face. Jake's heart contracted in response, heat flooding his body in a surprising rush. She might be pale, sick and disheveled—she might even be lying through her teeth—but she could still get through his defenses.

He tried to distract himself by checking out the window again. So far, the rain was holding off, although the clouds outside still looked threatening. He shifted so he'd have a longer view down the dirt road. No sign of Victor's van.

"Jake?" Mariah's voice floated from down the hallway.

He went to the bathroom and found her stripped to her panties and bra, revealing the ripe, lush curves he loved so much. But the pain in her eyes helped him get his treacherous body under control. "Did you hurt yourself?"

"I thought I should give the wound a better cleaning," she said through a wince.

Of course. He'd let his anger at her blind him to her needs. They might not get a better chance to flush out the gouge in her side. He reached into the tub and turned on both taps. "As soon as the water gets warm, get into the tub. I'm going to check outside again, just to make sure we don't have to make a run for it."

He dashed back out to the living room to reassure himself that Victor wasn't on the way, then returned to find Mariah standing in the tub, now completely nude.

He stumbled to a stop, trying not to stare. Trying not to want her so damned much.

"I wasn't sure what you wanted me to do." Her gray eyes locked with his, uncertain but also filled with a feral sort of sexual hunger he'd grown to anticipate over the course of their short but passionate marriage.

He had to clear his throat to speak. "We've got to flush the wound as much as we can." His hands trembling from the effort it took not to drag her into his embrace, he helped her into a kneeling position in the tub, her injured side positioned under the faucet. She gasped as the water hit the open wound, her fingers tightening like talons around his forearms.

"Shh, you're going to have to grit it out just a little bit, baby." He stroked her hair back from her pale, sweaty brow. Her eyes narrowed with agony, but she eased her grip on him, allowing him to make quick but thorough work of cleansing the jagged gouge in her side.

She was shuddering with reaction by the time he helped her out of the tub and wrapped a clean towel around her naked body. She leaned in against his chest, and he couldn't have stopped himself from wrapping his arms around her if he'd tried.

He stroked her hair lightly. "All done now."

"Do you think it'll help?" she asked, her voice muffled by the side of his neck.

"I think so. Can't hurt."

She finally stepped away from him, tucking the towel more tightly around her body. "I'm okay. I can take it from here. You should check and see if Victor's heading back."

He forced himself to leave the cozy, warm confines of the bathroom, even though a part of him ached to take her back into his arms. Settling in front of the living room window, staring out at the gray day, he realized that while he knew each exquisite inch of Mariah's beautiful body so intimately, in so many other ways she was a stranger to him.

WHY ARE YOU HOLDING on to the clothes?

Victor could only imagine what Karl would make of his decision to box up Marisol's clothes, along with her husband's, and stash them in a box next to his sofa.

He'd put the bags in the van. But not the clothes.

Karl would probably suggest some sort of Freudian obsession with her, as if there were anything remotely sexual about his relationship with Mariah.

Karl only understood the baser emotions.

He was going to get rid of the clothes. But first, he needed time to go through everything, make sure he didn't miss any identifying items in the pockets. Dumping the items in a charity box was smarter than just throwing them into the woods. In the charity box, they'd be a few items among many. In the woods, they'd be vital clues to what may have happened to a pair of missing persons.

But what if Karl got caught last night, dumping the truck and the boat? The sheriff might be on the way to the cabin right now, tipped off by Karl. The next car he passed could be a cruiser, lights flashing, barreling down the two-lane access road on their way to his house in the woods. What would he do if that happened? How could he stop such a disaster?

Victor had listened carefully to the morning news on

the radio, fearing the worst, but if Karl had been picked up by the police, the local stations hadn't found it newsworthy enough to report. More likely, Karl had managed to dump the truck and boat safely.

But that didn't really change the fact that sooner or later, when they realized just who this person named Mariah really was, they'd connect her to Victor and come looking.

He had to be very sure there was nothing in his house or the woods surrounding it that could incriminate him.

Including a box of clothes stashed next to his sofa.

Squaring his jaw with determination, he pulled a U-turn and headed back home.

IT WAS AMAZING WHAT A bath and a couple of extra-strength acetaminophen tablets could do for a girl. Mariah almost felt normal again. According to the thermometer in the first-aid kit, her temperature was down to around 100 degrees—high, but not scary. Her clothes were blessedly dry, for the moment at least, and the hardy waterproof overcoat she'd packed in case of bad weather during the tournament would keep the bulk of the rain off her when they had to leave the house.

"You look like you're feeling better." Jake's warm voice drew her attention to the doorway leading from the hallway into the living room.

He'd changed into a clean tan T-shirt and a pair of olive drab trousers he liked to wear when fishing. The shirt was well worn and a little too small, emphasizing the breadth of his chest and the well-toned muscles in his upper arms.

He'd probably had the shirt since he was much younger. He hated to throw things away, even when they were past their usefulness. It was one of his more frustrating—but charming—quirks. Right now, that little bit of familiarity gave her hope they could get out of this mess and find some way to get their marriage—their lives—back on track again.

She wanted to believe it, anyway.

"I do feel better," she admitted, walking toward him, pulled by an overwhelming need to close the distance between them, both physical and emotional.

"I didn't find a phone anywhere in the back of the house," he told her, turning away to pack his damp cast-offs at the bottom of the box with hers. The attempt to keep his distance was obvious. "It's possible he doesn't own one. He doesn't seem like the kind of guy who'd have a lot of people to call."

"He might have a cell phone he uses exclusively," she suggested as Jake crossed to the front window to check the road again. "He wasn't a big fan of phones back in the day, either. Talking on the phone unnerved him somehow. I think he didn't like not being able to read people's faces when he was talking to them." Again, she found herself drawn toward him, moving to stand beside him at the window.

"Is he the paranoid type?" Jake asked thoughtfully, looking down at her as her arm brushed his.

"A little. Yeah."

He didn't say anything else, but she could see his mind working behind his sharp blue eyes.

"I packed some food while you were in the bathroom," she added, filling the dead air. She showed him the canvas drawstring laundry bag she'd found in one of the cabinets and filled with pantry items. "I tried to take stuff that was in the back of the pantry so maybe he wouldn't miss it right away. I got peanut butter, crackers, raisins, bottled water, canned soup—we can't carry too much with us, but we won't have to go hungry for the next few meals."

He took the bag of food from her, his lips curving in a hint of a smile. "You never have liked having an empty stomach, have you?" Almost immediately his smile died, and the look he gave her was pained. "I guess, given your background, that makes a lot of sense, huh?"

"It's a luxury to have enough to eat," she murmured. "The sad thing was, there were people out there—churches and charities and all kinds of agencies—who'd have fed us good, hot food any time we needed it. But when your mother's more interested in getting drugs than feeding her kid—"

Jake raised his hand to her cheek, his thumb brushing over the curve of her chin. Closing her eyes, she leaned into the caress, overcome by how much she'd missed his touch.

When he dropped his hand away, she felt like weeping. Opening her eyes, she found he'd taken a step away, his gaze averted toward the window. Her heart breaking, she cleared her throat. "Do you think we have time to look for the binder a little more?"

Jake's gaze turned to meet hers, bright with urgency. "Actually, I'm not sure we have time to get out the back door before Victor walks in the front one."

Mariah hurried to where he stood, following his gaze. Outside, Victor's van advanced quickly up the muddy road, less than a hundred yards away. Her entire body went cold.

"Put the clothes back," Jake urged.

Mariah hurried to the box of clothes and pushed it back in place by the sofa with her foot, wincing as the action pulled at her injured side, while Jake locked the front door.

"Let's go!" Jake grabbed her hand and pulled her with

him toward the kitchen. "There's a back door—I spotted it earlier from outside. I think it's just off the kitchen."

He was right. There was a mudroom just off the kitchen—probably where the back door was located. She followed Jake into the small enclosed porch, skidding to a stop when he pulled up short and growled a succinct profanity. She peered around him and saw why he'd stopped.

The back door was padlocked shut from the inside.

"Oh God." Mariah moaned, fear making her legs tremble so violently that she wasn't sure how much longer she could stand.

"Come on." Jake pulled her with him into the hallway.

"What are you doing?" she whispered as he tugged her back into the living room. "He'll be in here any minute, Jake!"

"I know." Letting go of her hand, Jake threw open the door to the basement and plunged down the steps. "Come on!"

Her pounding heart in her throat, Mariah followed.

Chapter Ten

The box sat where Victor had left it, tucked between the sofa and the wall in the living room. With a sigh of relief, he picked it up and carried it out to the porch. Outside, full morning had dawned, rosy in the east, a potent reminder that he was losing precious daylight backtracking this way.

But what could he do? He couldn't go back to jail. Four years in that hell hole had nearly broken him.

He could fight eyewitness testimony, if Jake and Mariah escaped. He'd successfully painted her as crazy and volatile before. Her husband might be a harder sell, but Victor might have a fighting chance.

But if the cops connected him with evidence, he'd be done. He had to stay ahead of the evidence.

After putting the box of clothes in the cargo hold, he closed the door and started around to the driver's side, his gaze skimming across the front of his house.

He stopped mid-step. Something wasn't right.

Squinting, he tried to figure out what was giving him pause. Everything seemed as he'd left it, rickety and spare. He'd been meaning to fix the sagging eaves, give the place a little more dignified look. The sad, droopy porch was a depressing reminder of how much he'd lost since Marisol Mendez walked into his life and turned it upside down.

He used to have a real house. A real life. A purpose. She'd been part of the purpose, his greatest accomplishment.

He should have known that, beneath the veneer of civilization he'd managed to paint her with, she was still the little gutter snipe he'd snatched off of Bourbon Street and tried to give a life.

He needed to put her out of his head. She was spending too much time there as it was.

He looked at the porch, inch by inch. The rocking chair was there, the pine wood weathered almost beyond recognition. The rain barrel sat in front of the porch, dark with age. It had been half full the day before, but now he could see the water level from where he stood. The overnight rain had added several inches to the level.

What else? There was something else not right—

Victor's eyes settled on the edge of the porch. There was nothing there but the slightly warped wooden railing. But something should be there, he realized. The watering can that usually sat there was no longer on the edge of the porch.

He wasn't sure why he noticed the absence of the plastic container. He never used it. It had been here when he moved in, and he'd never gotten rid of it, thinking he might plant pansies later in the year.

He scanned the yard, thinking the watering can might have been blown away the night of the tornado. Had he seen it since then? He couldn't remember. He'd been in a hurry to grab breakfast the morning after. Then he'd seen Marisol on the news. That had been quite the distraction.

He scanned the yard one more time, just to be sure his eyes weren't deceiving him.

They weren't. The watering can was nowhere to be found.

"Did he leave?" Mariah asked, her voice barely a whisper. She sounded as if she wanted to believe it was true but couldn't quite bring herself to do so.

Jake strained his ears for sounds upstairs. They'd heard the front door open and footsteps moving around on the floor above. A soft scraping noise that Jake suspected might be the sound of the cardboard box of clothes being pulled from its cubbyhole between the sofa and the wall.

After a pause, there were more footsteps and the sound of a door closing.

Then nothing.

"I think he decided to come back for the clothes," Jake said quietly. "I really don't know why he didn't take them in the first place. Maybe he forgot them."

"So he's gone now?" Mariah sounded more hopeful than before.

"Maybe." There were no windows in this basement cellar, only solid, grimy stone walls. Jake had been afraid to turn on the light, in case Victor spotted the glow under the door, so all the light they allowed themselves was the flickering flame of the butane lighter. In the faint glow, Mariah's face looked drawn and shadowy, her eyes huge with fear.

He wanted to comfort her. But there was a mean little voice in the back of his head whispering that it was her fault they were in this mess in the first place, even though he knew such thoughts weren't fair.

She wasn't the only one who'd made a mess of their marriage, was she?

He'd done his part.

God, he hated feeling trapped and powerless. He hated knowing he'd spent the last three years in the dark, at the mercy of Mariah's secrets and lies, a willing dupe.

Willing because he had his own little secrets to hide,

and the Mariah he'd married had never once tried to ferret them out of him. It was one of the things about her that had appealed to him most.

He just hadn't anticipated she was keeping her own secrets.

Knowing the full story of her life, he could understand the choices she'd made. Maybe more than he understood some of his own choices.

"I wonder if he hid his scrapbook down here somewhere," Mariah murmured.

Jake eagerly latched on to that idea, tired of wallowing in his sense of betrayal. "When you found it before, it was in the basement, right? Back where you and he used to live."

"Right." Mariah peered around them. "It was hidden. I came across it trying to find a way out. So I don't think he'd keep it in plain sight."

Jake lifted the lighter to spread the light as far around the room as he could. The cellar was cluttered and dank, full of junk Jake was pretty sure had been here since long before Victor moved in, including a jumble of pots and metal tubing in the corner that bore a rich patina of age and use, giving Jake a pretty good idea how at least one of the previous homeowners had made his living.

He hadn't had much of a chance to look around the place earlier, when Victor was trying to imprison them down here. The basement didn't take up the full width and breadth of the house. It seemed to end short, as if whoever had dug the basement had grown tired of the job about halfway through and simply bricked up the unfinished dirt wall with leftover stone.

A few of the stones had fallen away, revealing patches of hard-packed dirt behind the facade. Some of the dirt patches were larger than others, he realized. Perhaps large enough to admit something the size of a binder?

He crossed to the wall, shining the lighter across the dirty stones. There seemed to be about four inches of space between the stone masonry and the packed-dirt wall.

"What are we looking for?" Mariah asked softly, her voice unexpectedly close. Her warm breath curled over the skin of his neck, sending a tremor rippling down his spine.

"I think Victor could put something into this space between the wall and the dirt behind it," he answered, dragging his mind back to the search for the binder.

"Wouldn't it drop all the way to the ground, out of reach?"

She was right. He lowered the lighter, looking for openings far enough down the wall that whatever Victor chose to hide inside would be easier to reach.

There. A slab of river stone about the size of a laptop computer lay on its side on the basement floor, revealing reddish brown dirt behind it. Jake hunkered down beside it, peering behind the stone. "I think I see something—" He stopped short at a sound upstairs.

Mariah clutched his arm, her grip urgent. "Was that—?"

He nodded, gazing up at the stairs. The front door had just opened.

VICTOR LET HIMSELF IN the house, stopping in the open doorway to listen. The house was silent, the only noise the faint *drip-drip* of water from the leaky kitchen faucet.

Karl, he thought. Karl had been playing him since this mess began, manipulating him, taunting him. His palm still stung where his Smith & Wesson had ripped up the flesh when Karl shot it out of his hand. His back ached from lugging the bags from Jake's truck the night before. All because of Karl.

He made a circuit of the house. Nothing seemed out of place, although the bathroom looked cleaner, somehow, than he'd remembered. There was a faint soapy scent as well.

He started toward the tub when a sound distracted him. He froze in place, listening.

He heard a faint series of *hiss-pop* noises coming from outside the house. His whole body went cold with dread, and he backed out of the bathroom, his hand reaching behind his back to close over the snub-nosed Taurus 605 tucked into the waistband of his jeans.

He walked slowly to the front window and looked out. Parked next to the van was a dark green truck emblazoned with the crest of the Mississippi Department of Wildlife, Fisheries and Parks. A stocky man in his late forties emerged from the driver's side door. Dressed in a camouflage jacket and olive drab uniform pants, he looked around the property as he approached the front door.

Victor couldn't let him come inside.

He hurried to the door and opened it, stepping onto the front porch. The Taurus felt heavy against his back.

The conservation officer came to a stop. "Hello there."

"Can I help you with something, Officer?"

"Just checking around, making sure we didn't miss any storm damage. Everything okay here?" The officer's gaze skimmed past Victor, settling on something behind him.

Victor turned, following the path of his gaze, and saw the two bullet holes in the siding. His stomach seized into a hard knot. He knew, with bleak certainty, that when he turned back to look at the conservation officer, he'd be staring down the barrel of a gun.

He couldn't let them take him alive.

Moving fast, knowing he couldn't possibly beat the officer to the trigger, Victor whipped his gun from his waistband, whirled and aimed it at the conservation officer, ready to fire.

The man stared back at him in utter surprise. He hadn't even drawn his weapon.

Victor's mind reeled with shock, his finger trembling on the trigger. He'd just incriminated himself, and for what?

For nothing at all. He'd let his own fears, his knowledge of his own crimes, escalate the situation to critical.

His hand shook on the gun grip. He wasn't used to firearms, didn't like the concussive kick or the stinging smell of gunpowder burning his nose. He hadn't even wanted a gun, much less two of them, but Alex had insisted he keep weapons on hand for protection. Alex couldn't afford to see Victor in custody again, either, he supposed, given what Victor knew.

Alex never used a gun himself, preferring his blades.

"Don't do anything foolish," the conservation officer said carefully, raising his hands. "I don't know what you think I'm up to, son, but—"

"Shut up," Victor growled. He needed to think, and he couldn't think with this idiot trying to play Dr. Phil.

He couldn't let the man go back to his SUV and call it in. He had to shoot him. Now.

But his finger wouldn't move on the trigger.

This was crazy. He wasn't afraid of death. Or making people pay for their sins. He wasn't afraid of stopping people who were intent on thwarting his plans.

He'd proved his determination on a Hattiesburg street four years ago.

Don't be afraid of the gun, Vic. Be a man. The memory of his father's hard Louisiana drawl filled Victor's ears. Suddenly, there was a snapping sound, like a nail gun being fired, followed by an explosion of breath from the conservation officer. The officer's eyes widened for a second, boring into Victor's. Then the man crumpled to the ground, blood spreading around him in a darkening pool.

Victor stared at the gun in his hand. It hadn't moved.

Footsteps squelching through mud drew Victor's gaze to the side of the house. Karl walked slowly toward him, his rifle slung over his shoulder, the sound suppressor still fitted to the end of the rifle's barrel. He looked down at the conservation officer's body, then back at Victor.

"This is why Alex chose me instead of you," he said softly, pride shining in his eyes. "Because I'm not afraid to take the shot when it's necessary."

Victor stared at him, drowning in hate.

"DO YOU THINK HE'S GONE AGAIN?" Mariah whispered, huddling close to Jake. They'd heard footsteps moving around overhead for a few seconds, then a sudden flutter of steps leading toward what sounded like the living room area. The door had opened and shut. They'd been listening for more sounds ever since.

A faint smacking noise filtered in from somewhere outside the southernmost basement wall. It sounded strangely familiar, though Mariah couldn't place it.

But the instant tension in Jake's body suggested he knew what they'd just heard. He wrapped his arm around Mariah's shoulders, pulling her closer, and backpedaled toward the center of the cellar.

"What was that?" she asked.

"High-powered rifle with a sound suppressor," he answered.

Just like the day before, when someone from the woods had shot the gun right out of Victor's hand.

"Do you think someone shot Victor?" she asked, horrified and hopeful at the same time.

"I don't know." Jake's gaze roamed around the cellar, as if looking for something.

"What are you looking for?"

"I keep thinking there must be a way out of here besides those stairs. A bolt hole of some sort—"

"We've been looking around this basement for a while now. Surely we'd have seen—"

Dropping his arm from around her, Jake extinguished the lighter, plunging them into utter darkness.

She reached out for him, needing the contact again, her body humming with reaction to the sudden sense that the world around her had disappeared. "Jake?"

"Just a second," he murmured, his voice reassuringly close. She edged closer to him until her arm bumped into his. To her relief, he didn't move away from her.

Darkness smothered them, thick and somehow tangible. But after a few seconds, the first faint light filtered past the unrelenting blackness—a pale glow emanating from the top of the steps, where a tiny sliver of daylight filtered in from the upstairs under the basement door.

Jake shifted his position until his back brushed up against hers. "Well, would you look there."

The butane sizzled to life again, the glow bright to her dilated pupils. Mariah turned and found Jake gazing toward a blank stone wall.

"What?" she asked, not understanding.

He caught her hand in his warm grasp and led her over to the wall. "Here, hold the lighter for me." He handed her the lighter. "Put your thumb there to keep the butane flowing."

She held the lighter while Jake started running his hands over the stones. "What did you see?"

"Light," he answered simply, placing his fingers over one of the large river stones set into the wall. Planting his feet firmly, he gave a sharp push.

To Mariah's amazement, a section of the wall began to swing outward, revealing a steep stairway rising upward from a small, square cement landing. Light poured into the area from somewhere at the top of the steps.

"How did you know?" she asked as Jake stepped into the cramped landing to have a look around. "That there was a door, I mean. That's why you turned off the lighter—to see if there was light coming in from anywhere else, wasn't it?"

Nodding, he came back into the basement and took the lighter from her. "See that over there?" He gestured toward a pile of debris in the back of the basement.

Mariah couldn't make much sense of it—a grimy, old boiler pot, a tangle of copper tubing—but Jake was looking at the mess with a grin on his face.

"It's junk," she said, trying but failing to see what he seemed to see in the jumble of debris.

"It's the makings of a moonshine still." Jake waved at the pile of junk again. "Crude, definitely homemade, but I'd be willing to bet it could produce quite a bit of alcohol when you got it going."

"What do you know about moonshine stills?"

"I'm an auxiliary deputy in Chickasaw County, Alabama, sweetheart. I've busted a moonshiner or two in my time." Taking her hand, he led her out the door into the tiny landing area. "I'd also bet this door leads up to the mudroom. I saw a door on the other side of the mudroom earlier, when we were trying to go out the back door, but we were in too big a hurry to stop and see where it went." He started up the stairs.

She fell in step, just behind him, glad for the rough

wood railing set into the side of the narrow stairwell, as each step sent a shock of pain racing through her injured side.

The stairway emerged into a tiny laundry room, where an old, battered washing machine took up most of the area. There was a hookup for a dryer but no appliance. A plain wood door stood closed, but a large window shed cloudy daylight into the laundry room.

Jake tried the window. It didn't seem to budge.

Mariah reached into the plastic sack where she'd stored the supplies she'd nicked from Victor's kitchen and produced a steak knife. "Try running this along the paint seal," she suggested.

The warm look Jake gave her made her knees wobble. He took the knife and turned back to the window. Running the blade along the paint seal, he sent flecks of dried enamel dancing in its path. He wiped the knife on his jeans and handed it back to her. "Let's give it another try."

This time, the window opened with a creak that was loud enough to make Mariah's hair stand on end.

"No time to worry about noise," Jake murmured, shoving the window up all the way. He hauled himself over the windowsill and out to the ground below. Gazing at her through the window, his expression apologetic, he patted the window sill. "It's going to hurt like hell, baby, but you can do it."

Mariah looked around the laundry room for something to give her a leg up to the window. There was nothing.

"Here," Jake said.

She turned to find him holding a paint can up in the window. She took the can—empty, to her relief—and set it on the floor. Standing on top of the can, she had more leverage to haul herself out the window and into Jake's waiting arms.

She clung to him for just a moment, not ready to move away from his warm embrace. She felt his breath stir her hair and for a second, she felt as safe and comforted as she'd ever felt in her life. But that moment ended all too soon, as Jake gently set her away from him. "Crouch low, below the windows. I want to see what's going on."

"We should just run," she protested softly.

"Victor could be dead," Jake pointed out. "We could be running from nothing now."

"Except whoever shot him," Mariah whispered.

Jake took her hand and led her to the corner of the house. Setting their supplies at their feet, he took a quick look around the corner. "Clear," he mouthed silently.

Leaving the bag there, they crept quietly down the side of the house toward the next corner. He let go of Mariah's hand and moved forward, past the corner, keeping low. Mariah peered around the edge of the house and saw they were next to the front porch. Jake was sheltered from view by the wooden structure.

He pointed to a gap in the pine lattice hiding the underside of the porch. Moving on hands and knees, he crawled through the gap into the shadow recess beneath the porch.

Mariah wasn't sure whether to stay where she was or follow. But the sound of squishy footsteps moving around in front of the porch made her mind up for her. She dropped to her hands and knees and scuttled after Jake.

The ground under the porch was damp but not muddy. It smelled of age and decay, but she kept her eyes on Jake, held her nose and scooted up beside him.

Shadows crisscrossed his face, but they couldn't obscure the look of fierce anger twisting his handsome features. Mariah followed his gaze and had to clamp her lips together to suppress a gasp of horror.

About ten feet in front of them, a man in a dark green uniform lay in a muddy pool of gore.

From her vantage point, she could see only feet and legs, moving around the body with deliberate steps. The shorter, stockier set of legs had to be Victor's. He walked with the faintest of limps—a leftover from his days playing high school football, or so he'd told her. Knowing what she knew about him now, she doubted he'd played team sports of any sort.

The man with the slight limp bent and grabbed the dead man's arms, confirming Mariah's guess. She bit her lip, hard, as Victor's head came up, his eyes seeming to meet hers for a heart-stopping instant.

Victor dragged the body toward the back end of a dark green truck just visible beyond the back of his van. The other set of legs moved around the van, the upper part of his body just out of sight. What Mariah could see of him, however, revealed a younger man, lithe and athletic.

He disappeared around the van. A moment later, Mariah heard the sound of a car door opening. She couldn't see the front of the truck, but she guessed Victor's unknown accomplice had opened the door.

"Put him in the back and cover him with the tarp back there. I'll take care of the next part," the accomplice said, in a light, surprisingly cheerful voice. "As always. You stay and clean up the mess you made."

Victor hauled the body onto the truck bed. It hit with a stomach-turning thud. Mariah turned her head, burying her face in Jake's shoulder.

"We have to go," Jake whispered as the truck engine roared to life. "Victor's got to clean up the blood, which means he'll go around the house to get the hose."

He'd see their bag of supplies if she and Jake didn't get to them first. Then he'd know they were here.

Mariah scurried to the narrow gap in the lattice work and emerged into the damp grass, ignoring the screaming pain in her side. She'd pay for all this activity later, but she didn't have the luxury of going weak.

Jake joined her as they ran at a crouch toward the back of the house. He grabbed their bag of supplies, tucking it close to his body so it wouldn't rattle around, and grabbed her hand.

They ran full tilt for the shelter of the woods.

Chapter Eleven

The ground underfoot was still soft from two days of rain and tangled with new undergrowth taking nourishment from the waterlogged soil, making Mariah long for a foot-path through the woods. But Jake assured her that the more treacherous the ground beneath their feet, the better. "He may be looking for us to stick to more beaten paths, the way we did last night."

Jake was right. Victor had almost found them before just by taking the path of least resistance. The zigzagging trek northeast was more like the path to poison ivy and stubbed toes.

Once they'd entered the woods behind Victor's house, Jake had forced her to slow down, warning her that crashing through the underbrush would only draw attention and make them instant targets. It had been hard to resist the adrenaline-fed urge to run, but Jake had held her hand the whole way, sharing his calm determination to reach relative safety without revealing their position to Victor or anyone else who might be hunting them.

Mariah's watch hadn't survived her fall into the creek the day before, but by her estimation, they'd been walking through the woods for at least ten minutes. It was slow going, the obstacle-strewn terrain forcing them to wind around trees and clumps of bushes until it sometimes felt that they were backtracking as often as they were advancing.

Jake drew to a stop and handed her a bottle of water from the canvas laundry bag he carried on his back, his arms threaded through the nylon cord drawstrings to create a makeshift backpack. She untwisted the cap and took a long, grateful swig.

"You want to rest a bit?" he asked.

The concern in his eyes was both gratifying and alarming. "I'm keeping up—"

"You are. But you should be in a hospital, not hiking for miles through the woods." He looked down at the side of her shirt. "Let me take a look at the bandage."

She hissed with pain when his hand brushed her side as he pulled up the hem of her flannel shirt to check the bandage. "Victor's going to find the paint can and know we were inside the house. He's probably out here looking for us right now."

"You're not bleeding," he murmured, lowering the hem of her flannel shirt over the bandage.

"I'll consider that a win," she said drily.

A hint of a smile played at the edges of his lips. "He was bound to notice the sudden influx of wet towels in the clothes hamper. All we could really hope for was a head start."

"We need to get out of these damned woods," she growled, gazing at the lush vegetation closing in the land around them.

"We can try going more north than east if you want." Jake picked up their bag of supplies. "We can't risk taking the dirt track back to the main road—"

"No, Victor goes that way. He could be on us before we could run," Mariah agreed.

"But we could parallel it awhile. We'd reach the road

eventually. And you know, if we head east, we might luck into civilization even sooner. Maybe someone else has a place in these woods." He narrowed his eyes, laying his palm against her cheek. His hand felt blessedly cool. She closed her eyes, leaning into his touch, unable to stop herself. Any minute he'd take his hand away, and she'd feel the full impact of their estrangement all over again.

But he let his hand linger. "You feel a little feverish."

She opened her eyes, praying for real concern in his eyes, a sign the connection between them wasn't permanently severed. She could almost see the struggle going on in his mind, between the shared history of the last three years and the lies on which the relationship had been based in the first place.

She drew away, unable to watch his inner battle play out across the canvas of his handsome face. "I'm okay. You don't have to worry about me."

"I do worry."

She dared another quick glance. His expression was wary but also full of concern.

The hint of tenderness in his eyes hit her like a truck. Tears burned hot in her eyes, blurring her vision until the woods around her melted into watercolor greens and browns. She took a hitching breath. "I'm so sorry, Jake. I'm sorry I put you in this position—"

"Shh." He twined his fingers in her hair and drew her into his arms, his breath warm against her temple. "We can sort through all of this later. Right now, I think you need to take a break. Just for a few minutes."

"I'm holding you back." Her throat ached with regret. "You should go on without me."

"Stop it, Mariah." He caught her arms in his hands, his grip unexpectedly strong, and stepped away from her. "We have a lot to talk about, I'll grant you that. But if you think

I'm the kind of man who'd even once consider leaving you here in the woods to fend for yourself just so I could get away, then you really don't have a clue who I am."

She didn't know who he was, she realized. Not the way she should. She didn't know whether he was really happy spending his days guiding fishermen to bass hotspots and giving two days a week to the Chickasaw County Sheriff's Department, or if he wanted something else out of his life.

She never let herself ask those questions—because she'd always feared he'd ask those same kinds of questions of her. The last thing she'd wanted from him were questions, for obvious reasons.

Their marriage had been lived entirely on the surface.

They'd never discussed having children. Never talked about moving to a bigger house. Never talked about growing old together and what kind of future they envisioned for themselves ten or twenty or fifty years down the road.

She'd stayed in her job working as Jake's sister Hannah's assistant at the marina, the same job she'd taken three years ago when she and Jake first met, because it was income and a way to stay busy, not because she thought it was the most challenging and interesting use of her time. And she'd never once told Jake that's how she felt.

Before the last two fateful days, Jake thought she had earned a bachelor's degree in psychology, because that's what she'd told his family to explain her knowledge of hypnosis, a parlor trick she'd pulled out once at a Cooper family get-together without thinking it through.

After all, she could hardly explain that she'd really learned the trick from a wily, old con artist she'd met when she was eighteen and living on the streets of New Orleans, could she? Not without telling them the rest of her sordid history.

She hadn't told Jake the truth about almost anything in her past. She'd cobbled her history together with bits and pieces of her favorite books, fashioning a lawyer father, now deceased, after Atticus Finch and a beloved mother, also deceased, after Marmee from *Little Women*. The memories of Texas she'd shared with him were a patchwork quilt of real memories and scenes from the travelogues she'd read in Victor's vast library.

She wondered where those books were now. She hadn't seen them in the forest shack.

"What are you thinking?" Jake asked softly as the silence between them thickened.

She said the first thing that came to mind. "What did you want to be when you grew up?"

His eyebrows twitched his surprise. "A superhero."

She couldn't hold back a soft huff of laughter. "It was the cape, wasn't it?"

He grinned. "Nah, just the saving hot chicks part."

Her smile widened, then faded as she realized just how revealing his answer really was. "That's what you thought you were doing with me, wasn't it? Saving the poor single mom trying to scrape together enough dimes to take care of her kid. Is that why you asked me to marry you? To solve my problems?"

His grin disappeared as well. "I wanted you." His eyes darkened with hunger. "Still do."

In a flash so fast, so fierce that she could barely breathe, desire swallowed her whole, inhabiting her body until she ached. This, she understood. This attraction, this yearning for each other, had never been a problem. She'd felt the tug of his masculinity the first time she laid eyes on him. It had caught her by surprise, a flash of feeling coming from a place inside her that she'd thought dead and gone.

Jake moved closer, bending his head toward her, his intent beyond question. He was going to kiss her.

And she was going to let him.

As she rose to meet him, opening her mouth to his kiss, he threaded his fingers through her hair and drew her head back, deepening the kiss the second their lips met. Their tongues met in a slick, sweet tangle, leaving Mariah feeling shattered and weak. She grabbed his wrists, holding on tightly just to stay on her feet.

When he tore his mouth away from hers and drew back to look at her, she struggled to breathe, her heart jackrabbiting against her breast bone.

She felt as if she were standing in the middle of a storm, whipped by the maelstrom of desire bearing down on her like a whirlwind. "We've never had a problem with this part of our marriage, have we?"

"I think it may be the only thing we ever fully shared with each other." Jake dropped his hands to his side, giving her room to step back if she wanted.

She didn't want to step back. She wanted to throw herself back into his arms and let him drive away the fear and the sadness and the shame with the heat and power of his body on hers, skin to skin. If only making love could be enough to drive away all the rest of the garbage that had piled up between them without either of them really noticing.

"Let's get moving," Jake said, already moving away.

Gathering up the strength she had left, she followed.

BY NOON, BILLOWING BLACK clouds had swallowed the last of the blue in the sky. Lightning sparked in the west, punctuated by low, grumbling thunder, and the temperature dropped noticeably, exacerbated by a wind strong enough to whip the collar of Jake's windbreaker against his face.

Hiking out of the woods was taking longer than he'd thought. He was a good outdoorsman, having grown up roaming the woods that blanketed the land around the family home on Gossamer Lake. But there was a difference between making your way around woods as familiar to you as your own face and finding your way out of unfamiliar territory with an injured woman in tow and a couple of killers dogging your steps.

"What is that?" Mariah asked.

At first, Jake was struck more by the thready sound of her voice than what she'd said. He turned to find her lagging behind a couple of yards, her wan complexion and furrowed brow suggesting she'd reached her limit.

She was gazing toward the east, her eyes narrowed and one arm raised, pointing.

Following her gaze, he spotted a large clump of kudzu vines about eight yards away, forming a natural, box-shaped topiary. There was something under the strangling vines, too small to be a house, but whatever lay beneath the vines might provide them some semblance of shelter against the coming storm.

"Stay here and rest a bit," he said. "I'll check out what's beneath the kudzu."

"No, I'm okay." Her jaw clenched, as if taking another step took every ounce of strength she had, but the look she gave him brooked no further argument.

He slowed his pace, staying close to help her navigate the tangle of underbrush between them and the vine-covered structure just visible beyond the trees. As they got closer, he saw weathered, gray wood peeking out between the dark-green leaves of the kudzu vine.

It must be some sort of storage shed, he realized, abandoned to the smothering embrace of the kudzu, although what it was doing in the middle of the woods, far from any other structure, was a puzzle.

Soon, however, he saw that the shed was positioned in what might have once been a small clearing. The trees in this patch of the woods were saplings or young trees, no more than six or seven years old. There might have been a house here once, or some other larger structure, which would explain the shed.

Mariah pitched forward suddenly. He caught her before she hit the ground. "Are you okay?"

"Yeah, I just stumbled over something—" She peered at the ground, kicking at the thick kudzu vines that covered this section of the forest floor. Her foot pushed aside the tangle of leafy vines to reveal the remains of a house foundation.

The concrete still showed signs of dark patches of soot. Suddenly, the whole picture became clear.

"There must have been a house here once," Jake said, now able to see the square outline smothered by the kudzu. "Probably burned down to the foundation and nobody bothered to build here again."

Taking Mariah's hand, he detoured around the foundation and reached the shed. Tugging at the vines covering the shed wall, he saw that underneath, the structure seemed to be well constructed. Solid weather-treated pine comprised the shed itself, and a tin roof was just visible through the vines near the top of the kudzu sculpture.

Uncovering the door of the shed, Jake found it swollen shut from all the rain, but he managed to pull it open with a little effort, revealing a dark, cramped interior.

"Wait here," he directed Mariah, pulling the supply bag from his shoulders and fishing out a flashlight. He darted the light around the shed, surprised to find that the inside was mostly dry despite the recent heavy rains.

Faint daylight entered the grimy windows of the empty shed, and, to his relief, no light peeked through the tin roof overhead. The roof had apparently held up well under the stresses of the mercurial south Mississippi climate.

Or maybe the shed wasn't as old as he thought. Kudzu was notoriously aggressive, and without inhabitants to beat back its approach, it wouldn't have taken that long for the invasive vine to swallow the shed whole. The house could have burned as recently as five or six years ago, for all he knew.

Only a few weeds had invaded the dirt floor, mostly along the wall bases, where small spaces between the pine slats would have allowed windblown seeds to take root in the soil. Kudzu tendrils had also snaked their way across the floor, giving them a rich, green carpet.

Jake shined his light around, looking for snakes, which would be more active now that winter was over. Timber rattlers were all over the woods this time of year, and this abandoned shed would have made a decent winter home.

Fortunately, the shed was snake-free, though there were enough spider webs lacing the walls to give his sister Hannah permanent nightmares.

Other than the spiders and the carpet of kudzu, the shed was empty. Whatever tools had been here once were long gone, either taken by the property owners or filched by local kids or thieves who happened upon the place during their hikes.

Jake shrugged out of his jacket and laid it across the dirt floor, then beckoned for Mariah to join him. It was a tight fit; the shed was no more than eight feet by eight feet. But it was shelter against the fat raindrops that had already started falling through the canopy of leaves overhead.

"Wow, a dry place to rest," Mariah murmured. "What did we do to deserve this?"

"Let's rest awhile. The rain's probably going to stick around a bit, so we might as well stay dry until it's done." Jake waved at his jacket and held out his hand to her.

Mariah gazed back at him a moment, not moving. Her eyes were luminous, lit up as if from within. Those quicksilver eyes had been the very first thing he'd noticed about her, even before her gorgeous caramel skin and sexy curves.

"Do you love me?" she asked.

The question threw him completely. How was he supposed to answer? *Yes, but I'm not sure I love you enough to get past this mess?*

"I'm sorry." She looked down at the ground. "That was such an unfair question."

He shook his head. If their relationship had any hope of surviving, a hard dose of the truth was called for. "I love the woman I married," he answered. "But you aren't that woman. That woman never really existed, did she?"

She bit her bottom lip and sat down, looking up at him as if to invite him to sit as well.

He sat cross-legged across from her, trying to make himself relax. He hadn't planned to have this conversation yet.

Apparently, neither had she, for she changed the subject immediately. "You hungry? I'm hungry."

"I could go for some peanut butter and crackers," he admitted, lightening his tone deliberately. No matter how much her lies had hurt him, he didn't believe she had kept her secrets maliciously. And they were still stuck in the woods together, trying to find their way to safety, for the foreseeable future.

"I wonder how Micah's doing," she murmured as she handed him a sleeve of crackers and reached into the bag again, returning with the jar of peanut butter she'd taken from Victor's pantry. "Probably hasn't even missed us." Her voice cracked a little.

"Ah, he misses you. He always wants his mommy to read him a bedtime story." Jake took the plastic knife she handed him from the supply bag, his heart swelling a little at the thought of his stepson. Micah was three now, chunky and happy as a pig in mud most of the time. He was already starting to read simple words and knew the alphabet by heart. He looked just like Mariah, all dusky skin, raven hair and quicksilver eyes.

God, Jake loved that boy. Micah called him Daddy, and that's how he felt about the child, biology be damned.

Fear flickered in the center of his chest at the thought of losing Micah. What if he and Mariah couldn't figure out how to fix what her lies had broken?

Jake's peanut butter cracker caught in his throat. He washed it down with a swig of water from the bottle they shared and set his food aside, turning to face her, feeling queasy. "You didn't want me to adopt Micah."

She looked up, her expression startled. "I never said—"

"I brought it up, more than once. You always tabled the discussion for later." His heart sank when she looked away, guilt flitting furtively across her face. "You thought it would be disloyal to Micah's father."

She forced her gaze back up to meet his. "Not disloyal. Just—it would be like severing the final tie."

"You're still in love with him."

"I'll always love him." The naked pain in her eyes was hard to look at. "If you want me to stop, I'm sorry. I can't give that to you."

It wasn't what he wanted. He couldn't expect it—he'd seen his brother J.D.'s constancy, over a decade after his wife's murder, and knew that real love never died. He also knew from watching his sister Hannah with her husband

Riley, who'd been a grieving widower when he met her, that a second chance at love could be just as powerful as the first.

So why hadn't he and Mariah made it happen?

"I don't know what I want from you," he admitted. "Except honesty, I guess."

She wrapped up their leftover food, her movements slow and deliberate. She put the food back into the bag and set it aside, as if clearing out anything that might sit between them.

Her eyes lifted and met his, blazing with intensity. "Here's the honest truth. There's a lot I don't know. About who I am now, what I want or even what I feel." She reached across the space between them, running her fingertips down the plane of his stomach until her fingers caught in the waistband of his jeans.

"Mariah—" he growled as her palm pressed intimately against his sex.

"I've had enough talking. It's getting us nowhere." She rose to her knees and moved forward until she straddled his lap. "Let's try something else."

He wanted to protest. If he tried, he could come up with a dozen reasons why giving in to her seduction was a crazy, dangerous idea, not the least of which were a couple of murderous psychopaths roaming the woods outside, desperate to cover their tracks. But the minute Mariah's soft lips moved urgently over his, Jake forgot everything but the surging fire in his blood.

She hissed when he snagged her bandage while starting to pull her shirt over her head. He drew back for a moment, cursing himself for forgetting her wound.

"No," Mariah whispered, nipping the tendon at the side of his neck. "I'm okay." Leaving the shirt on, she threaded her fingers through his, urging him onto his back. Bending, she kissed his lips, lightly, teasingly, over and over again until he thought he was going to explode.

Then her lips slid down the curve of his jaw and suckled the side of his neck, sending heat flooding his veins until he felt himself begin to unravel.

Frantically removing only the necessary pieces of clothing, they made love with fierce urgency, leaving Jake barely able to catch his breath. The more he demanded, the more she demanded in return, throwing her head back and abandoning herself completely, like a wild creature finally unfettered, allowed to run free.

Jake gazed up at her, stunned by her feral beauty. A whirlwind of conflicting emotions hurtled through him in cadence with his pounding heart.

He was making love to a woman he'd never seen before.

Chapter Twelve

A shrill ringing broke through the white noise of the rain-storm outside Victor's house, rattling his nerves. He didn't have a land line, and his own cell phone, a cheap, pre-paid job he'd bought soon after his release from prison, sat silently in his pocket. Unnervingly silent, since he'd been expecting—dreading—to hear from Alex ever since Karl drove away with the conservation officer's body.

Following the trill, he found the cell phone under the sofa. It must have dropped from the bag before he'd taken it to the truck. He picked it up and saw that the display once again read Gabe Cooper.

Victor let the phone ring, each shrill sound sparking a tremor down his spine. Finally, the sound died away and the room was silent again, save for the patter of rain on his roof.

Victor crossed to the front window and looked outside, his gaze focused on the patch of ground where the conservation officer had fallen. He saw only grass and mud; what the water hose hadn't washed away, the downpour outside had taken care of. The area might not stand up to forensic soil-sample examination, but the cops wouldn't have reason to look here for a crime scene, even if the conservation officer had called in his position before he got out of the truck.

Karl had said he was going to dump the truck a mile or so from where he'd gotten rid of Jake's truck and boat. Victor didn't want to know where. The less he knew, the better.

The cell phone rang again, impossibly loud. Same caller. Same number. When it stopped ringing this time, Victor removed the battery and wiped both pieces down with the hem of his shirt, removing any prints. He put the phone and battery atop the box of clothes he planned to drop at the local charity box.

Another ringing sound made Victor jump. He stared at the cell phone, half expecting the empty case to be lit up, taunting him. Then he realized the sound was coming from his own pocket.

Alex's name glowed on the display. Dread burned in Victor's gut, but he didn't dare ignore the call. "Yeah?"

"I just spoke with Karl." Alex sounded deceptively pleasant. Victor knew better. No doubt Karl had painted the latest debacle in the most unflattering terms possible.

"I told you to lie low. I can't afford more mistakes from you. I don't want to come to the conclusion that our friendship was a mistake." Alex's tone was that of a disappointed father, equal parts anger and sadness. Victor wished he could believe the implied affection underlying the words, but Alex's distance since Victor's incarceration seemed more and more like betrayal.

He wasn't sure why he wanted back in the man's good graces.

Because you miss the excitement, a quiet voice in his head answered for him. *The power you feel when you're around him.*

"You have the rest of the day to tie up loose ends," Alex said, all forbearance gone from his voice. "If you haven't, I will give Karl carte blanche to do so for you. Understood?"

Tension rose in Victor's chest. "Understood."

He hung up the phone, shaking.

"STILL NOTHING?" His brother Luke's voice, unexpectedly close, sent a little shudder through Gabe Cooper's system. He looked up to find his older brother standing at the bait shop counter, worry darkening his gray eyes.

"No answer," Gabe answered tersely, trying not to let his worry spill over into his voice. He had played along with the reassurances of the family that it wasn't unusual for Jake to be so late getting back home from a trip away.

His older brother J.D. had suggested that maybe Jake and Mariah had stopped at a motel overnight rather than driving straight through to Gossamer Ridge. After all, they couldn't have slept much the night before, with an F5 tornado blowing through the town around them. Or maybe they'd decided to stay another day after all, and hadn't called to let them know yet.

All very logical, Gabe had to concede.

But he was Jake's twin. And while he'd never much bought into the whole twin mystique, he couldn't shake the feeling that something was very wrong with his brother.

"Did Aaron ever get through to the Buckley police to see if cell service was restored?" Luke asked.

"He said most service was restored by this morning," Gabe replied. "I just tried Jake's cell. It rang through instead of going straight to voice mail."

"Sounds like he's got service, then," Luke said. "Maybe he couldn't get to his phone in time to answer."

Gabe nodded, trying to believe it. Maybe they were sleeping late in some interstate motel and didn't answer the phone in time. But he didn't buy it.

He picked up his cell phone and dialed the number again. "Damn it," he muttered. "Straight to voice mail."

"Maybe he's screening," Luke suggested.

"He'd know we'd be worried he's not here yet," Gabe answered firmly. "Something's gone wrong."

RAIN RAPPED A STACCATO rhythm on the tin roof over their heads, echoing the frantic drum beat of Jake's heart. Mariah lay draped across his body, covering him with her warmth. She made a soft, grumbling sound when he moved her hair away from her face to check her for fever.

"You okay?" he asked cautiously.

She lifted her head, gazing at him with pleasure-drugged eyes. "I'm good. You?"

He wasn't sure how to answer.

Her brow furrowed at his hesitation. "What is it? Do you hear something outside?"

"No." He eased her to the ground beside him, needing distance to gather his thoughts in some sort of coherent order.

Narrowing her eyes, she seemed to shrink back from him. "You're scaring me, Jake."

He was scaring himself. His mind filled with the image of how she'd looked before, when she'd given herself so completely to their lovemaking. He'd never seen anything more beautiful.

Or so alien to him. That woman had been a stranger.

He tugged on his jeans, feeling vulnerable. As if taking her cues from him, she pulled on her own jeans, wincing as the movement tugged at her side. Shivering a little, she wrapped her arms around herself, palpable fear in her eyes.

He hated being the one who put the fear there, but he

owed her the truth. There'd been enough lies between them already.

He cleared his throat. "When we first met, you didn't take me seriously. Remember?" She'd treated his come-ons as jokes, though he'd meant them as seriously as he was capable of being at that time in his life.

"You were coming on a little strong." A smile graced her lips briefly. "It was hard to believe you meant it."

"I meant it. Sort of."

Her eyes flickered. "You didn't think I was a goddess?" Her tone was deliberately light, but he could see a hint of pain lurking in the glistening depths of her eyes.

"I thought you were a pretty woman who'd had a bad day and could use a pick-me-up. And if we ended up having a fun time together, that was okay, too." Jake tucked his knees up to his chest, feeling a little sick about what he was admitting. "Usually, in those kinds of circumstances, there'll be a laugh or two, some nice dates, maybe kissing, maybe more. But it always goes away, sooner or later. I expected that."

"But I didn't go away." She spoke carefully, as if the words she was about to speak had the power to break her. "And you regret it now."

It took all his strength to keep from pulling her into a hug. But it wouldn't mean what she wanted, any more than the sex they'd just shared had meant what they'd both wanted it to mean.

He wasn't sure he even knew what he wanted it to mean. That was the real problem, wasn't it? He never looked closely enough at what he really wanted from her—hell, from life—to know why he did the things he did.

He didn't like things to be difficult. Easy Come, Easy Go had been his motto for a long time now. Life was a lot less disappointing when you didn't have many expectations.

"I don't know who you are, Mariah. I've lived with you, slept in your bed, touched and tasted every inch of you, but I still don't know who you are."

"I'm not that different—"

"You are. Don't you see that?" He released a frustrated sigh, feeling more inarticulate than he'd ever felt before. He was the guy with the gift of gab, or so his brothers had always accused, but somehow, he couldn't find the words to say what he wanted—needed—to say.

"Jake—"

"I'm not the guy you married, either. I don't think I ever was." He knew, even as he said the words, that he was making no sense. But somehow, understanding dawned in Mariah's eyes anyway, along with a thin film of tears.

"You were lying, too." Oddly, she didn't sound surprised.

"To everybody, not just you. I was even lying to myself."

"About what?" She asked the question in the tone of voice of someone who knew what the answer would be. Apparently, she just wanted him to voice his realization aloud.

He took a breath and took the plunge. "I was lying about who I really am." Now that he could see the truth, it seemed painfully clear. "The Jake Cooper who laughed his way through life, never feeling anything too strongly or looking at anything too closely—he wasn't real. He wasn't any more real than the Mariah Davis who walked into the marina office that day, pretending to be a widowed mother just looking for a job."

"I know." Tears spilled down her cheeks. "I've always known. You weren't really happy. You weren't really unhappy. You just didn't let yourself feel much of anything at all."

He stared at her, surprised how perfectly she seemed to understand his feelings. "Why didn't you ever call me on it?"

She dropped her gaze to her lap, where her right hand was twisting the simple gold band on her left ring finger. "I didn't want you to examine any of your choices too closely."

Of course not. Jake watched her play with the ring, remembering the day he'd put it on her finger. He'd felt, even then, the unreality of what he was doing. But he'd been thirty years old and it had seemed as if getting married and being a father were the kinds of things he was supposed to be doing at that point in his life.

And he *had* been crazy about Mariah and her son, as much as he'd ever been about anyone, though now he saw that her most appealing attribute had been how bloody undemanding she'd been.

"You never asked me what I wanted from life, Mariah. Or even what I saw myself doing five or ten years down the road. You never expected me to change or grow." He laughed bleakly. "It just took me until now to realize it's because you didn't really care, one way or the other."

"I couldn't *let* myself care," she corrected softly. "About any of it. Because everything goes away. It's better not to get too attached to anything, you see? I mean, I couldn't really help it with my son. He was my reason for getting up in the morning and going out to face the world." She pushed back a strand of dark hair that had fallen across her face. "But I couldn't let myself have expectations from you. You gave me a home and a family. A place to belong. I didn't think I had a right to want more."

"So when I chased you, you just let me catch you." Saying the words out loud hurt more than he'd expected. "You became a blank canvas for me, let me paint you to be the kind of woman I wanted. Patient, undemanding, doing whatever I needed you to do, being who I needed you to be—my God, you must have hated every moment of it."

She shook her head. "No." She sounded as if she meant it, but he couldn't believe her. It made no sense.

"You work at my folks' marina because I like having you close by. You let your hair grow long because I prefer it that way. You wear green all the time because I think it looks great on you—" He ran his hand over his eyes, feeling sick. "And I let you do it because it was easier for me that way. My God, you must despise me for that."

She closed her eyes for a moment, pain etching lines in her pale face. But when she opened her eyes, they blazed with a fierce light. "I thought I might, but I don't. You're not as selfish as you think you are. You did make compromises."

"Nothing hard."

"I never asked you to make any hard choices." She put her hand on his, her grip soft but strong. "You're strong enough to go after whatever it is you want, and you're strong enough to bear it if you fail. I know you are. You'll do the right thing, no matter what it is. I just didn't give you the chance to prove it. To me or to yourself. I'm so sorry about that."

He looked at her through narrowed eyes, aching to believe her. He was disgusted by what he'd just figured out about himself. Disgusted and terrified. He'd always thought the distance he put between himself and other people, the walls he built, were a sign of toughness. They kept him strong. Untouchable. But he was neither.

This small, vulnerable woman could hurt him. Had hurt him. He'd brought it all on himself with his cowardice.

And if the look of sorrow in her eyes meant anything, he'd hurt her, too. All because neither of them had been brave enough to tell the damned truth, whatever the consequences.

"So why?" she asked softly.

He frowned, not following. "Why what?"

"Why are you the way you are? You said I didn't ask before. Well, I'm asking now."

He stared at her for a long moment, trying to formulate an answer in his emotion-fogged brain. It had to have started with Coach Morrison, hadn't it? That was the last time he'd felt innocent and hopeful.

"In seventh grade, my best friend was Darryl Morrison. His father coached our little league team. I thought he was the coolest guy on earth."

"Did the coach—" Her voice faltered. She stopped and started again. "Did he do something to you?"

"No," he said quickly. "Nothing like that. I just—I don't know, I idolized him. I was at an age where kids start thinking of their parents as boring and embarrassing, but they find everybody else's parents cool and heroic. That's how I felt about Mr. Morrison and his wife Ann."

"And they didn't turn out to be heroes?" she guessed.

"I walked in on Mr. Morrison cheating on his wife with the teenage babysitter in the bedroom at Darryl's house."

"Oh, dear." She made a sympathetic noise.

"I know it sounds stupid. I should have gotten past it—"

"You idolized your friend's father. And at that age, you probably even had a crush on the babysitter. Seeing them both that way let you down—"

He nodded. "I didn't know who to tell. So I told Darryl."

She winced. "How did he take it?"

"He told his mother, and Mrs. Morrison said I was a nasty liar and wasn't welcome there anymore. I haven't seen him since then. As far as I know, the Morrisons are still together."

She put her hand on his. Her touch was warm and soft, but he felt oddly threatened by it. He pulled his hand away.

She drew her hand into her lap. "So you decided after that it was easier not to care about anyone or anything?"

He nodded, feeling foolish. "I know it's nothing compared to what you went through—"

"It was bad enough," she said firmly. "But maybe you should stop letting it control your life."

"The way you've stopped letting your past control you?" he countered defensively.

Her expression flickered as if he'd struck her. He regretted his words immediately but couldn't take them back.

Mariah cleared her throat. "Where do we go from here?"

He didn't know. Rather than answering, he reached for the bag of supplies and pulled out the first-aid kit. "Let's take a look at your wound."

She didn't move for a moment, gazing at him with wide, emotion-darkened eyes. But she finally scooted closer, lifting the edge of her shirt.

The cleaning they'd been able to do at Victor's house had helped. The angry red color had faded to pink, and there were already signs of healing beginning along the edges of the torn skin. "It looks better," he said aloud.

She released a soft breath. "It's not hurting as much."

"That's good." He pulled the first-aid supplies from the belly of the supply bag. "This will sting."

She winced as he ran an antiseptic wipe over the edges of her wound. He quickly replaced the sting with cool, soothing antibacterial ointment, covering the gouge with a fresh bandage.

"All done," he said, sitting back. Cool air filled the space between them.

She pushed to her feet and crossed to the small shed window, peering out through the film of grime and the tangle of kudzu at the rainy woods outside the shed. "I wonder if we should start gathering up animals two by two."

He joined her at the window. Rain had removed some of the dirt on the warped pane, and gaps in the kudzu gave him a pretty good view of the lush woods. The patches of sky visible through the trees remained a deep, angry gray, though the lightning storm seemed to have passed.

"We need to head out of here soon," he murmured.

She turned to look at him. "I wish we'd never come here."

"Me, too," he agreed, although he wasn't sure he meant it. If they hadn't come here, he wouldn't know the truth. As painful as it was, it was better to know. Wasn't it?

"I just want you to know—" Her voice faltered, forcing her to clear her throat and start over. "I want you to know I was going to tell you everything when we got home."

"But not before you saw Victor again."

She looked down. "No. But I'm not sorry you know."

He tipped her chin up with his fingers. "Are you sure about that?"

Her gaze leveled with his. "We've been living a beautiful lie for the past three years, but it was still a lie. It was—corrosive. Don't you think?"

He couldn't argue with her. Somewhere, deep down, he'd always known their whole relationship was little more than smoke and mirrors. It had been entirely too easy to be real.

"But maybe it doesn't have to be," she added, her voice

so soft he could barely hear it over the drumbeat of the rain on the roof. "Maybe we could start over, do it right."

His chest tightened with emotion, a potent blend of fear and longing. "What if we fail?"

"What if we don't try?"

A flicker of movement outside the shed caught Jake's eye. He pulled Mariah back from the window, tucking her behind him. It took a second to make out what he'd seen through the muddy rain sheeting the window.

It was a deer. A doe, slender and delicate-looking, her ears flicking as a hard rain pelted her. She seemed to gaze right at him through the window, then turned and bounded off, the movement as graceful as a dancer.

"Just a deer," he said, peering after the animal until she disappeared from sight.

"Could have been something else," Mariah said in a low, strangled voice, her eyes wide with fear. "It *will* be something else, sooner or later."

"My family's bound to be looking for us already." Even as he said it, he knew they might not have enough time to wait for his family to track down all the leads. God only knew what Victor had done with his truck and the boat. If someone happened across the vehicles a county over, they'd be searching in all the wrong places.

He had to get himself and Mariah out of here on his own, before Victor or his unknown accomplice found them.

But running on empty wasn't a good idea, either.

"I think we can rest here a little longer," he said, making a decision. "We haven't slept worth a damn in a couple of days, and if we keep pushing ahead like this, we're going to start making big, costly mistakes."

"Victor's probably already found out we were at the

house," Mariah protested. "He'll find the paint can or figure out there are things missing from the pantry."

"And that'll make it look like we're hunkering down out in the woods somewhere."

She shot him a desperate look. "Isn't that what we're doing?"

"The woods are big. He's going to search our last known location first, and that's near the creek." At least, Jake hoped so. "We're at least a couple of miles from there, in the opposite direction."

Mariah slid down the wall to a crouch, pressing her hands over her face. "I just want to get out of here."

"Can't argue with that."

She looked up at him. "Are you sure it was just a deer out there?"

Since he couldn't answer yes with any certainty, he shook his head. "I'll go take a quick scout of the area."

She shook her head. "It's pouring rain out there. I'm just being paranoid."

He hunkered down beside her to look her in the eye. "I don't think there's any way to be too paranoid in our situation." He rose and picked up his jacket where it lay on the floor. Dusting it off, he slipped it on over his T-shirt. He crossed to the dirt-clouded window by the shed door, scanning the woods. The view was better here, since he'd torn away several of the kudzu vines from the front of the shed. He saw nothing moving outside. "I'm just going to check the perimeter. I'll be right back."

Opening the front door of the shed only far enough to allow him to slip out, he scanned the woods ahead and to his immediate left and right, then edged his way to the eastern corner of the shed. He stayed still for a moment, listening for any unexpected noises in the woods audible over the driving tempo of the rain. Hearing nothing, he crept around the corner.

Repeating the same pattern of waiting and listening, he made a complete circle around the shed, finding no sign of intruders. He reached the door and was about to go back inside when he heard a faint hum, like the sound of an engine, moving through the woods about a hundred yards distant.

His heart thumped hard and fast against his ribcage. It sounded like an all terrain vehicle. He hadn't seen anything like that around Victor's place, so it wasn't likely to be him. And hadn't they watched his accomplice drive off in a conservation officer's truck? It could just as easily be a local, doing a little property assessment after the tornado. A local who could get him and Mariah to safety before Victor found them.

On instinct, he started following the sound of the ATV.

The engine noise seemed to be coming from the north, heading south. Jake was between the rider and his destination, but he had to move at a noisy but fast clip through the woods to reach the point where he and the rider would intersect before the ATV arrived. He needed to hide until he knew whether or not the newcomer was friend or foe.

He heard the engine noise coming closer. They were still nowhere near anything that resembled a road, but the trees in this area were thinner, the ground relatively flat and free of the heavier undergrowth that tangled through the woods to the east. Maybe the road was closer than he thought?

He found a small thicket of wild hydrangeas, the wide leaves and conical blooms giving him the cover he needed to see the ATV rider before the rider saw him. The engine noise was much louder now, revving now and then as the rider gunned the engine to move over the rough, uneven ground.

Jake spotted the vehicle finally, moving in a shallow zigzagging pattern as it avoided larger obstacles like bushes and hillocks. The rider was dressed in a leather jacket and jeans, his head and face obscured by a shiny black helmet with a full, tinted face shield. But it was too tall and slim to be Victor, he saw with relief.

He started to move out from behind the bushes, stepping as far as the edge of the thicket, when he saw something sticking up behind the rider's back. It was a rifle with a sound suppressor attached to the end of the barrel.

It was Victor's partner in murder.

Chapter Thirteen

Jake slipped back into the shadows of the hydrangea bushes, his heart hammering, as the sound of the ATV moved past him, heading deeper into the woods. Then, with shocking suddenness, the noise died into silence.

Jake froze.

The sound of something moving in the woods ahead filtered past the rush of rainfall, forcing Jake to move out of his safety zone. He stayed as far behind the bushes as he could as he peered ahead, to where the ATV had gone.

He could see nothing from this vantage point, but the sounds of movement through the underbrush was still audible, heading away from him.

Heading east, toward the shed.

Toward Mariah.

Jake waited a few seconds, then started to follow, moving as silently as he could while keeping pace with the man crashing through the woods ahead of him.

If this man found Mariah before Jake could stop him, there was no doubt in his mind what the man would do.

He'd kill her as surely as he and Victor had killed the conservation officer outside Victor's house.

JAKE HAD BEEN GONE too long. Without a watch, she couldn't be sure how much time had passed since he slipped outside the shed, but from the time she started to worry until now, she'd counted slowly to three hundred. That was another five minutes.

Where had he gone?

She'd wondered, briefly, if he'd decided to walk out on his own. Leave her behind as she'd suggested earlier, since she was only slowing him down. But she couldn't imagine Jake doing something like that any more than she could picture him turning his back on his family. If nothing else, Jakes loved Micah as if her son was his own. He'd never leave Micah's mother unprotected and injured.

He'd never leave anyone unprotected and injured. It wasn't the kind of man he was.

So wherever he'd gone, he'd had a good reason for going.

She had taken advantage of the time alone to wash up, glad to have a moment to compose herself alone. Making love with Jake had shaken her far more than she'd expected. In a way, it had felt as if it was their first time, full of surprises and unexpected revelations.

She supposed in a lot of ways, it *was* their first time— the first time she'd been completely herself with him, nothing held back. It had been the first time he'd looked at her and known the truth of who she was and where she'd been in her life.

And it was the first time she'd completely lost control with anyone. Including Micah Davis.

They had been young. Immature in some ways. Probably as unprepared for the life they'd planned to embark on together as any young couple not long out of their teens.

Mariah was only four years older now, but those four years had been filled with a lifetime of hard lessons and deep regrets. She felt older than twenty-five. Older and wiser.

She had spent so much time trying to protect herself from further hurt that she hadn't realized what was happening behind those walls she'd built.

She'd been falling in love with her husband.

Jake believed she didn't know who he was, but he was wrong. She'd known all along that the real Jake Cooper was the guy hiding behind the jokes and the cheerful demeanor. She'd seen the moments of truth that occasionally slipped from beneath the mask, like the anxiety he felt for his family and the recent dangers they'd faced. She'd seen his secret envy when Hannah, Sam, Luke and Aaron each found the happiness that had eluded them too long, and his hidden fear that they would lose, sooner or later, the new love they'd discovered.

She had known she wasn't the kind of wife Jake needed. He needed a woman who'd challenge him, love him, force him to work through his fears and doubts and be as strong on the inside as he was on the outside.

But she couldn't afford to be anything but the wife he wanted, someone who wouldn't look too closely at him or challenge his beliefs about himself and the life he was living. So that was the wife she'd been.

But no more. Jake may not ever love her the way she'd come to love him, but the very least she owed him was the truth. About herself. About how she saw him.

And then they'd work through everything together.

She heard the sound of a motor, distant but moving closer. Her heart skipped a beat, then began to race.

Pushing to her feet, she crossed to the window and peered out. The rain had let up in the last few minutes, improving visibility. But she still couldn't see anything but trees, bushes and undergrowth.

She opened the shed door slowly, listening. The sound

of the engine was louder now, though still some distance away. It sounded as if it was coming from the west.

She started to slip outside but stopped, looking back at the dim interior of the shed. She didn't want to step foot out of this place without the supply bag. It might be heavy and even painful, tugging as it would on her injured side, but she couldn't risk being trapped outside without it. What if that engine was Victor's van?

She hoped—prayed—it was someone who could help them get to safety. But if it wasn't, she needed to be prepared.

Mimicking the way Jake had used the straps to fashion a backpack, she threaded her arms through the drawstrings, gasping as the full weight of the supplies bent her spine. It was much heavier than she remembered. But not unbearable, she decided with a lift of her chin.

She started out in a careful zigzagging pattern, trying to remember the tracking lessons Jake had shared with her over the last couple of years when they'd gone hiking or camping. He was a natural, instinctively understanding the land, the trees, how nature worked and what to do to keep from disturbing it unnecessarily.

She, on the other hand, had grown up in Houston, one of the country's largest cities. Even after she'd headed east, she'd ended up in New Orleans, trying to keep her head above water without resorting to selling her body. Long nature walks had been the last thing on her mind.

She'd have been better off trying to sneak up on someone in the French Quarter, where alleys, courtyards and small, dark little shops would have served her well as points of escape and camouflage.

So it didn't come as a complete surprise when she almost stumbled right into the path of a tall, slender man dressed in a leather jacket, jeans and a black motorcycle helmet, carrying a rifle propped against his right shoulder.

The only thing that saved her from discovery was the cover of a kudzu-strangled stand of broken tree stumps, apparently snapped by a tornado or straight line winds some years past. Like the shed and the house foundation they'd stumbled across earlier, the trees had been swallowed whole by the fast-growing vine, creating a forest topiary.

This particular viny sculpture formed a picket-fence shape, the snapped trunks close enough together that the vine had tangled in on itself, bridging the gaps between the stumps. The broken trunks towered twenty feet high, but the draping kudzu between them created a wall of green stretching not quite half that height, but plenty high enough to wall Mariah off from the man in black leather striding through the woods less than six feet from her hiding place.

She hunkered deeper in her verdant shelter, peering through the tiny gaps in the vines for a better look at the intruder. Even beyond the rifle, there was something ominous about the black helmet—who wore a helmet to hike the woods? A normal person—a person with no ulterior motive—would have left the helmet with the motorcycle or whatever vehicle had made the sputtering noise she'd heard in the woods. Or removed it and carried it in his hand, improving his ability to see in the rainy woods.

This person was hiding his identity.

He walked past the last broken trunk and into the open. If he'd turned around just then, there'd be no way he'd have missed seeing her flattened there against the wall of kudzu. But he didn't turn, moving forward into the woods at a determined gait, a man on a mission.

She caught a glimpse of rusty brown on the back of his

pant leg, and her heart skipped a beat. The build was right, and the stain could be blood—was this Victor's mysterious accomplice?

Could he know about the shed? If he looked for them there, he'd see that someone had recently torn away several of the vines from the shed front. He'd know they'd been there. He'd know he was looking in the right place. How long would it be before he tracked one or both of them down?

A new, terrifying thought assaulted her, sucking the air from her lungs. What if Jake was on his way back to the shed right now? Or worse, what if he'd already run into the black-helmeted man and lived to regret it?

He wouldn't have let the man get this close if he were able, would he? He'd have stopped him, or died trying.

For a second, her mind seemed to shut down, snagged in place by that terrible thought. Dread weighted her down, numbing all sensation except for a piercing ache right in the center of her chest.

What if Jake was dead? What would she do? How could she bear such a loss again, now that she knew just how damned much she loved him?

She had to find him. Dead or alive. If was alive, he might need her help. Or he might be in danger of stumbling onto the mysterious man stalking through the woods toward their hideout. And if he was dead—

The image of Micah's broken, bleeding body lying in the middle of a Hattiesburg road flooded her brain for the first time since it happened, ramping up her agony. She squeezed her eyes shut, as if she could block out the memory, but it came from within, relentless and horrifying. Only this time, she realized, it wasn't Micah Davis dying in her arms as she wrapped them around him, trying to will life back into his failing body.

It was Jake.

She dragged her eyes open, determined to fight off the paralyzing pain. The man in the leather jacket was almost out of sight, moving inexorably closer to their former hiding place.

If Jake had gone back there to find her gone, there's no telling what he might be doing now.

Occam's razor, Marisol. Victor's voice whispered in her head, a reminder of days long past when he was her teacher, not her tormenter. *What's the simplest answer?*

That Jake would never leave her. Either he didn't know about the intruder and he was heading back to the shed because that's where he expected to find her, or he knew about the intruder and was heading there to get her out safely.

Either way, she was going back to the shed.

JAKE HAD THE ADVANTAGE of knowing exactly where to find the shed where Mariah awaited his return. But the man in the black helmet, carrying the rifle over his shoulder, had the advantage of firepower and the resulting indifference to maintaining even a semblance of stealth. To keep from drawing the gunman's attention, Jake had to move quietly and quickly on a parallel path that took him through tangled underbrush that probably hadn't seen human feet for months, if not years.

So far, the combination of driving rain and carelessness on the part of the armed stranger had made it easier than Jake expected to keep pace. But keeping pace wasn't good enough. Jake needed to get ahead of the man and reach the shed in enough time to get Mariah out of there before they were discovered.

He wasn't going to make it. The man in the helmet slowed to a stop within fifty yards of the shed, his head cocking slightly sideways as if he weren't sure what he was seeing at first. Jake stopped, staying behind the man's line of peripheral vision. He crouched low, terror stealing his breath.

Mariah was trapped and had no idea what was coming for her.

Suddenly, Jake heard a twig snap behind him. Slowly swiveling his head, he scanned the woods for signs of movement.

There. A slight shudder of a wisteria vine climbing an oak tree about thirty yards behind where the man in the helmet stood pondering the kudzu-draped shed.

Jake circled slowly backward, angling so that he could approach the second intruder from behind. The last thing he needed was a blitz attack from the rear while he was trying to keep the rifleman from doing anything to hurt Mariah.

He was close to the trembling tree when the man in the helmet made a sudden move forward, toward the shed. Jake froze, racing through his options. He could go after the rifleman right now and take his chances on subduing him before he got a chance to fire a shot. But that would leave him vulnerable to whoever was hiding in the tree ahead.

Or he could see if the hider was the gunman's accomplice. It might give him leverage to broker a trade.

His heart told him to go after the gunman. But his head told him to play it smart.

This time, his head won. Keeping one eye on the man in the helmet, who had almost reached the shed, Jake moved in on the position of the person hiding in the trees.

At the shed, the gunman was taking a slow circuit around the building. Jake had to drop lower to keep from being seen, slowing his approach toward the wisteria-draped oak about fifteen yards ahead. When the gunman rounded the shed and slipped out of sight, Jake made his move.

He closed the distance between himself and the tree, not bothering with stealth at this point. The person hidden in the vines turned, sending the whole tree shaking.

Silver eyes met his, wide and terrified. His body went hot, then cold with relief.

Mariah's face lit up when she recognized him, a dazzling smile splitting her pale face. "Jake," she whispered.

He touched her lips to urge her to remain quiet. "We've got to get out of here."

VICTOR'S CELL PHONE rang again. Not recognizing the number, he almost chose to ignore it. But something in his gut urged him to answer.

"Yeah?"

"I think I found your fugitives." Karl's voice was low and singsong. "Or at least, where they were earlier today. Interested?"

Victor's heart thumped more rapidly against his ribcage. If Karl was right, he might finally end this two-day nightmare and get on with his life. Alex or no Alex.

"Of course," he said, grabbing a pen and a notebook.

MARIAH FELT AS IF SHE were snuggled into a warm, rock-solid cocoon, but she couldn't complain. The feel of Jake's body wrapped around her as they huddled in a tight crouch, waiting for the man with the helmet to pass their hiding place, more than made up for any momentary discomfort.

Jake waited until they heard the engine noise fire up and start moving away before he relaxed his hold on her. But she didn't try to move away from him, not wanting to leave the shelter of his body.

He stood, drawing her up with him. "Come on, let's get moving." He took the supply pack from her and looped the drawstrings over his arms, already moving toward the west. But Mariah couldn't seem to make her feet move. Her body was shaking too violently.

He noticed she wasn't with him about five yards away and turned back to look at her. "Mariah?"

"I thought you were dead." She could still feel the hard, hot ache in her throat from her earlier imaginings, still see her worst fears playing out in the darkness behind her eyes.

He walked back to her slowly, his expression sympathetic. "I was a little worried about you, too, baby."

The endearment unraveled her tightly wound control. Before she was even aware of moving, she was wrapped around his body, her face pressed against his chest so she could reassure herself with the steady, powerful beat of his heart. He wrapped his arms around her, his lips hot and sweet against her brow.

"We're okay," he whispered, and there was something in his tone that made her hope he might be talking about more than just their present danger.

She lifted her face to look at him. "Jake, you're still angry with me and I deserve it, I do. But I need to tell you—"

He pressed his thumb against her lips, stilling her confessions in mid-sentence. "When we get out of here, we're going to have a whole lot to talk about. But we have to hurry and get to the road."

A flicker of doubt stained her previous hopefulness. Maybe she'd misunderstood his concern for her safety, took it to be an indication of an epiphany similar to her own, when she'd realized she had fallen in love with him after all. But he was right—there was no time for talking.

The wind was gusting hard now, driving the pouring rain into them like stinging needles. The ground underfoot was softening so much that Mariah felt as if she were starting to sink into the earth with each step.

Jake said he thought they were close to the road. Once they reached the road, they'd be a lot closer to civilization and safety. Then they could talk about what the future held.

"I heard the engine moving north, so I think we're right in thinking the main road lies—" Jake's voice was swallowed by a loud cracking sound. A gust of wind hit Mariah hard, overbalancing her. She stumbled sideways, struggling to stay on her feet.

She lost the battle when Jake sudden grabbed her and flung her aside, sending her rolling down a slight incline. Pain ripped through her side, stealing her breath. Her ears filled with a loud whooshing sound, then a thud that made the earth shimmy beneath her.

She tumbled to a stop, finally, against the trunk of an oak tree. Tiny acorns dug into her back where she lay, gasping in pain.

She forced herself to a sitting position, staring wildly around her to see what had just happened.

A tree had fallen, a thirty-foot pine. It hadn't snapped, like the trees they'd sheltered under the day before, but fallen over completely, uprooted by the gusting winds. The top branches lay less than five feet away from where she sat.

But where was Jake?

"Jake!" She scrambled to her feet, the pain in her side already fading to nothing in comparison to the clawing terror rising up from inside to consume her. "Jake, answer me!"

"Shh—I'm here." His voice came from somewhere

nearby, but she couldn't see him at first. Then his arm rose from within a tangle of pine boughs about ten feet away.

She hurried to him, her heart pounding. She faltered to a stop as the full import of what she was seeing filtered into her stunned brain.

Jake was trapped under the fallen tree.

Chapter Fourteen

The cry was brief, muted by distance, but Victor knew Marisol's voice like his own. It had haunted his dreams for four long years, taunted him with her lies and betrayals deep in the night when he was too wound up or anxious to sleep in his prison bunk.

Anticipation twisted in his belly like a hungry snake. Karl had been right. The voice had come from the same direction as the old shed he'd come upon a couple of months ago, when he'd first leased the old shanty in the woods. He'd had a lot of time on his hands then, as now. Not much to do but explore the parcel of forest he now called home.

Karl had found evidence that the kudzu had been disturbed recently and figured it had to be Marisol and her husband. Now Victor had proof that Karl hadn't been lying, at least.

He was still a little worried, however, that Karl might be setting a trap.

Sure, if Karl really wanted him dead, he knew where to find him. He could have easily killed Victor right in his own house. Nobody would've come looking for him for days, maybe weeks, until the landlord started wondering whether or not he'd skipped out on his rent.

But Karl liked games.

The rain was relentless, driven in prickly sheets by powerful wind gusts. Victor had checked the radio for a weather report not long before Karl had called. New storms were blowing through the area for the next couple of hours, bringing strong straight line winds but not much threat of any more tornadoes.

He wondered if he could somehow use the storm to his advantage. It would be easier to avoid any unwanted inquiries from the cops if Marisol and her husband seemed to have died as a result of the storm.

There had been no stories on the radio news about the truck and boat being found. No news about the missing conservation officer, either, but it was early.

Victor still had time to make it all right.

But first, he had to find Marisol and Jake, and put an end to the threat they posed.

"Shh, don't yell. Someone could hear." Jake tried to hide the level of his discomfort from her, not wanting her to panic any more than she already had.

"How badly are you hurt?" she asked softly, trying to make her way through the prickly pine needles to see the damage, even though he could see how much she dreaded what she'd find.

"I don't think it's bad," he reassured her, truthfully. "I can move my legs a little, and it doesn't hurt that much." One knee felt badly contused, and he couldn't move it enough beneath the limb pinning him to the ground to tell if there was a substantial injury. But at least he could move it. He could still feel both of his feet. That was a plus.

"The limb won't budge?" Mariah gave it a tug, grunting softly as the limb trembled a little from her effort but didn't move from its position across his legs.

"No. I think there's a piece that dug into the mud like

a stake. It's not wanting to come up." Jake pushed hard against the large limb pinning him to the ground. He could feel it give a little, but he couldn't get enough leverage from where he lay to get it off of him. "If I had something to dig with—a large stick would do, I think—"

Mariah dashed away for a second and returned with a fallen branch from a hickory tree not far away. It had been down awhile, Jake saw, the leaves all gone and the smaller twigs branching out from the limb snapping away easily with a little effort. Most of the bark had been stripped, perhaps by deer or other foraging animals.

Mariah started digging at the mud around his legs, trying to create more space between the fallen branch and his limbs. When she spoke, her whisper was a little shaky. "Are you sure you're not just saying you're okay so I won't panic?"

"I promise." He took the stick from her, his attempt at a smile turning into a grimace as the twisting movement sent pain shooting through his knee. "I don't think I'm in any danger, but I really can't tell from here what the damage is. I can move. I'm not in a lot of pain unless I move a certain way, and even then, it's no worse than the last time I twisted my knee. I'm hoping that's a good sign."

He started digging at the ground next to him, hoping his better upper body strength would make the work go faster than letting her do it, but he couldn't get a good angle on it from where he lay on his back.

Mariah took the stick away from him. "I have a better angle, Jake."

He lay back, gazing up at her in frustration. It could take precious minutes to dig enough mud out from around his legs to free him. Time they didn't have. "We're not far from the road now. Maybe you should try going for help."

"I'm not leaving you here alone."

"You may have to."

The stick hit a rock, shaking Mariah's whole body. The rain made it hard to keep a good grip on the slick wood. He'd noticed that fact himself. She sat back on her heels for a moment to wipe the rain from her eyes. "Maybe so," she conceded, "but let's give this a little bit longer." She started digging again.

"I won't hold it against you if you go."

"I'd hold it against myself," she murmured.

He put his hand over hers. "This isn't your fault. Not all of it. I played a pretty big part."

She lost her grip on the stick as it hit another rock. Grimacing, she sat back on her heels again. "I know. But maybe you wouldn't have made the choices you made if I'd given you other options. You may not have ever asked me to marry you if you knew the truth."

He didn't know how to answer her. It was true; he might have made another choice if he'd known the truth. Or maybe, he'd have sucked it up and acted like a man, following the attraction between them to a deeper, more mature place than they'd gone. He just didn't know.

She looked a little hurt by his continued silence, but he didn't want to tell her a pretty lie. Not now that they were finally telling each other the truth.

"I can't keep my grip on this damned stick," she growled as the hickory branch slipped again. Wincing, she peered down at her palm.

"Splinter?" he asked.

"Yeah." She plucked it out with another grimace.

"Let me see," Jake said, reaching for her hand.

She laughed weakly. "Says the man under the tree."

"You may not have gotten it all."

"I'm okay," she insisted.

"Are you so sure about that?" A male voice carried to them on the driving wind.

Mariah's whole body jerked, overbalancing her forward. She caught herself on her hands and knees, scrambling around until she was facing the other direction. Jake twisted his upper body until he was lying half on his side. But it gave him a better view of the woods behind them, where he saw Victor Logan standing about twenty yards away, holding a small, snub-nosed revolver trained at the center of Mariah's chest.

Jake wriggled under the weight of the tree limb, desperate to get out before fear eclipsed his frustration. Fear would paralyze him further, and he was already vulnerable enough.

Victor took a few crunching steps toward them, a smile spreading across his dark face. "It's time we end this, don't you think?"

Jake wrapped his hand around Mariah's ankle, squeezing gently. She looked down into his eyes, her silvery gray gaze full of fear and regret. Then her expression shifted, her jaw setting and a strange new light filling her eyes.

Lifting her head, she pushed to her feet and faced Victor again, her shoulders squaring. "You're right. It's definitely time to end this."

Victor's gun hand twitched, but Jake saw that he didn't have a good grip on it, nor did he show the ease of a skilled gunman as he brought the barrel to bear on Mariah.

She held up her hands. "I'm over this, Victor. I'm over playing wife. You were right. I'm really not cut out for it. I should have listened to you after all."

Jake's stomach tensed as Mariah's words rang in his ears. Her voice was strong. Firm. Full of conviction.

As if she meant every word she'd said.

Victor's eyes flickered with surprise. "What are you trying to pull?"

Mariah scraped her wet hair out of her face, her expression fierce with frustration. "I just want to go back to where we were before. I've been living with this idiot for three years, laughing at his puerile jokes, and I've had all I can take."

She didn't look at Jake, so he couldn't read her eyes. But the haughty disgust in her voice was alien, a sound he'd never heard from her lips before.

Was it possible that was really how she saw him? He'd thought she must hate him, living with him all this time, pretending to be someone she wasn't. She'd assured him she didn't. But had that been the lie?

"You can't fool me," Victor insisted, although Jake could already tell he wanted to believe her. From what Mariah had told him about Victor, he was a guy who hated to lose as much as any psychopathic narcissist. Winning Mariah back from a younger, stronger rival like Jake would be quite a coup.

"No, I can't," she admitted, her voice trembling with regret. "I never could. I could fool myself, but not you."

Victor's gaze darted down to where Jake lay pinned beneath the tree limb, then back to her. "I should just shoot you now and get it over with," he growled, his words making Jake's heart take an upward lurch, until he saw that the angle of Victor's weapon barrel had already dropped off to the side, well away from Mariah.

Whatever she was trying to do, it was working. She was getting to him.

"You're not going to shoot me," she said firmly. "You're going to take me home with you. We both made mistakes. I'm willing to admit mine now, just like you admitted yours. I should have believed you when you said it was an accident when you hit Micah." For the first time since she'd squared her jaw and faced Victor head on, Jake heard a false note in her voice.

She'd been shattered by Micah Davis's death. Whatever else she might be up to, whatever she was saying that might hold a kernel of truth, there was no way she'd ever believe Micah's death had been an accident.

"What about him?" Victor looked at Jake again, his expression full of contempt.

"Leave him." Mariah took a few steps toward Victor, not looking back at Jake.

"What if he gets away?"

"His knee is broken. And he's pinned. He can't get away. He'll be dead of exposure before anyone finds him." She threw a quick look back at him, her expression cold. "An unfortunate accident caused by the storms. So sad."

Her voice was cold as ice, but her eyes blazed as they met his. In them, he saw all that she wasn't saying—the fear, the desperation and the fiery determination.

She was the Pied Piper, leading the snake away from Jake so he had a chance to get out of this mess alive.

GABE'S CELL PHONE RANG as he was ringing up a customer's purchase, startling the man.

Gabe thrust the man's change at him. "Sorry, gotta get this." He grabbed the phone off the bait store counter and found his brother Sam's name on the caller ID display. "Sam. Anything yet?" he asked eagerly.

Sam Cooper was a district attorney in Birmingham now, but he'd spent several years working in Washington, D.C., where he'd made a lot of powerful contacts. He'd offered to call in some old markers to get the information they were looking for. Apparently it had worked, for his voice went grim. "The cell signal from Jake's phone pinged off a tower about four miles from downtown Buckley, Mississippi."

"Buckley?" Gabe's heart dropped. "He and Mariah left Buckley yesterday before lunchtime."

"Apparently not," Sam said. "Or, at least, his phone didn't. Have you tried Mariah's cell?"

"She lost it when she went into the river rescuing that kid." Jake had told Gabe the whole story. "Something's wrong, Sam. This isn't just Jake being Jake."

"I called Kristen." Sam's wife, Kristen, was a detective with the Gossamer Ridge Police Department. "She's contacting the authorities in Buckley to check on accident reports or anything that might tell us where they are."

"That's not good enough."

"They're a little overwhelmed at the moment. The tornado did some major damage. Lots of people are still missing."

"So's Jake."

"Hard to convince the locals that he's more important than the families they're still trying to rescue," Sam pointed out with the calm, sane logic that made him the solid rock of the Cooper family.

But Gabe wasn't in the mood for calm, sane logic. "There's got to be something we can do."

"It'll take at least eight hours to drive to Buckley from here, but maybe that's what one of us should do—"

"It's only an hour or two by air," Gabe said, an idea forming.

"J.D.," Sam said, following Gabe's train of thought.

"Gotta go, Sam." Gabe ended the call, then pressed the speed dial button for his eldest brother, J.D.

After three rings, J.D. answered, a dying whine of machinery punctuating his greeting. J.D. was a boat mechanic who made his living providing maintenance and repair to the customers who moored their boats at the family's marina. But it was his occasional moonlighting job that most interested Gabe.

"It's me," he greeted his brother, dispensing with niceties. "Sam says Jake's cell phone pinged to a tower in Buckley. Looks like he never left the area, and nobody can reach him or Mariah."

J.D. released a low profanity. "Did anybody call it in to the local law?"

"Kristen's on it, but the locals are still swamped digging out from the tornado. Jake and Mariah aren't going to be a priority for them. It's up to us." Gabe clutched the phone more tightly. "Think you can borrow the chopper?"

"I DON'T BELIEVE YOU, you know." Victor's grip on her arm was tight and punishing, but Mariah could take it. She could take anything if it gave Jake a chance to free himself and get to safety.

"I know," she said aloud, struggling to keep pace with his angry stride up the dirt road. Jake had been right; they hadn't been far from the road at all. She'd nudged the stick she'd been using to dig closer to him before she left with Victor, trying to be subtle about it.

She hoped Jake understood what she was doing, but if he was so angry at her it gave him the strength to dig out, then so be it. As long as he managed to get away and go for help, she didn't care what he thought of her.

He was close enough to the road that, if he could walk at all, he could make it.

She had faith in him.

"But it must mean something that you're taking me with you instead of killing me," she added, trying to sound both fearful and hopeful at the same time. Funny how the time and distance from Victor had allowed her to understand him far better than she had during the years she'd been his unofficial apprentice.

His intelligence had been warped to serve his narcissism, his love of learning channeled into a petty, mean-spirited sort of self-absorption. He'd never had real affection for her, outside of how her eagerness for knowledge and her quick learning had reflected his abilities as a teacher.

He saw her as his creation, her accomplishments entirely due to what he'd taught her while her flaws were purely her own, defects in the medium rather than the sculptor's mistakes.

To the extent she could play on that vision of himself, and of their relationship, she had a fighting chance to stay alive until Jake found help or she herself could find a way to escape.

"I haven't decided what I'm going to do with you," Victor responded. "I'm not sure I did the right thing, leaving your latest conquest behind."

Panic rose into her throat, but she fought to hide it. "It's the right thing. He has family that will look for us, but they won't find him in time. He's badly hurt. He can't even move his legs. He won't last more than a day or so. And when they do find him, they'll think his death was an accident."

Even though she knew Jake's injuries probably weren't as serious as she was saying, it hurt to speak the lie aloud. Just imagining what might have happened, how much worse things could have gotten—could still get—was enough to send a wave of nausea wriggling through her belly.

"And what will you tell them of your part in the mess?"

"I'll tell them that we got separated when the truck broke down. He went off to look for help and when he didn't come back, I went to look for him and got lost in the woods myself." Her toe hit a rock sticking up in the muddy road, making her stumble. Victor tightened his grip to keep her from falling, surprisingly gentle once she was steady on her feet again.

But his touch still made her want to jerk her arm away and put as much distance between them as possible.

You can't let yourself think that way. You have to pretend he's still the guy you used to like and admire. She plastered a grateful smile on her face. "Thank you."

His eyes narrowed slightly. "The truck isn't where you left it. That story won't work."

"What did you do with it?"

"I didn't do anything," he said carefully, but she could tell he was lying. He also looked uncomfortable, and she got the feeling he didn't know where the truck was.

"Who's the guy who shot at you from the woods? Do you know?" She tried to keep her tone idle, as if she were just making conversation. If she tried to pump him for information about his mysterious accomplice, she might put herself in even more danger. She couldn't afford to alienate him any further. If he changed his mind and went back to kill Jake—

"Just someone I know. I guess he thought he was playing the part of the hero. When I informed him otherwise, he was appropriately abashed." Victor kept his eyes forward, as if concentrating on the uneven track ahead.

But Mariah realized he just didn't want to look her in the eyes. She suspected it had been Victor, not the shooter, who'd been humiliated by the encounter. But why?

Who on earth was the man with the rifle?

ON THE POSITIVE SIDE, Jake thought with a grimace, at least the pain in his shoulders and arms was making him forget how bloody much his knee hurt. He'd started digging like a madman the minute he lost sight of Mariah and Victor, but it was nearly impossible from his position to get any real leverage.

Meanwhile, though the wind had largely died down now, and the rain all but stopped, there were enough sporadic gusts to shake the trees overhead, spurring Jake's urgency to be free. One large limb of a nearby oak had already snapped off, scaring the hell out of him as he watched it plunge toward him, but lower branches of the tree had broken its fall. It now hung precariously on those branches, wobbling every time the wind picked up but holding in place so far.

Still digging, he felt a rock give way beneath his left calf, the one with the swollen knee. He wiggled his leg. His knee ached in protest, but he was able to move more freely now. Just being able to change positions felt like a miracle.

Overhead, the boughs of the oak rattled violently in the burst of wind. Jake looked up in time to see the broken limb slip off its perch and come hurtling downward.

He twisted his body sideways, dodging what he could. The limb fell less than two feet away, twigs slapping his face.

His heart galloping like a thoroughbred, Jake closed his eyes and released his pent-up breath, every nerve in his body jumping. He took a few more seconds to compose himself, then turned to push the fallen limb away from him.

It was sturdier than he'd thought it would be. He'd figured the limb must have been weakened by disease and rot to have snapped, but it felt as solid as a fence post.

Solid enough to use as a lever?

Jake looked down at the rock he'd managed to dig away from his legs and saw that it was larger than he'd realized, at least nine inches in diameter, and about four inches tall where it sat. Would that be enough height to work as a fulcrum?

He tugged at the rock, the jagged stone ripping at his blistered fingers, until it popped free of the fallen tree. It felt solid, igneous rather than sedimentary, which meant it would hold up to stress better than some rocks he might have found. He eyed the fallen oak limb again, wondering how heavy it might be.

He tested its heft and found it dense but not impossible to maneuver. He didn't need to carry it around with him; he only needed to push it into position to work as a lever to lift the fallen pine tree off his legs.

Gritting his teeth, he started stripping the larger limb of its branches and leaves.

Chapter Fifteen

Victor's house came into view sooner than she'd expected. The walk back hadn't seemed to take half the time she and Jake had spent going from the house to the kudzu-covered shed. Of course, they'd been picking their way through underbrush and around trees, trying to escape detection as well, while she and Victor had traveled openly on a relatively level and hospitable dirt road. Calculating, she thought they were less than a mile from where she and Victor had left Jake, and if she had to guess, the main road where they'd last seen their truck was probably another mile farther north.

Now she just had to figure out how to get away from Victor.

She wondered, as Victor led her up the porch steps, whether or not he'd figured out they'd been in his house earlier that day. They'd tried to clean up as much as possible, but it was impossible to hide things like wet towels in the hamper or food missing from the pantry. She also hadn't had a way to remove the paint can she'd used to climb out the window at the back of the house.

Of course, he might have been distracted by his murder of the conservation officer she'd seen him tossing into the bed of the poor man's truck.

"You're probably hungry," Victor said gruffly as he closed the door behind him.

The last thing Mariah wanted was food. But she played along. "I could use something warm. I bet you have some tomato soup. I know you love tomato soup."

He turned to look at her, his eyes narrowing. "We're not friends, Marisol."

"Not yet," she said, keeping an element of brightness in her voice. "But I remember what you taught me about perseverance. I don't give in easily."

He studied her silently for a second, then waved toward the kitchen with the hand that still held the snub-nosed revolver. She wasn't sure whether it was a deliberate warning that she was still his prisoner or if he'd simply forgotten he was holding the weapon.

In the kitchen, she eyed the knife block but didn't go for it. Victor would shoot her before she got there. She almost crossed to the pantry, in her nervousness, before realizing that she didn't want to tip Victor off to her earlier visit to his kitchen. "Where do you keep the soup?" she asked.

"In the pantry." He pointed at the door.

Mariah opened the pantry door only far enough to slip her hand inside and pull out a can of tomato soup. She hoped Victor didn't see far enough inside to notice there were items missing.

Victor took a seat at the kitchen table, keeping the revolver in hand. "There's a pan in the rack by the sink."

She picked up a saucepan from the rack and set it on the stove next to the can opener. "Maybe after lunch, we could read. Where do you keep your books?" She'd noticed, during her earlier, abbreviated tour of the house with Jake, that his vast collection of books, some quite valuable, wasn't anywhere in sight, though there were a couple of rooms she hadn't visited before she and Jake had to make a run for it.

"I sold many of the more valuable volumes to pay the lawyer." Victor's voice was low and grim. "Others are in storage. Probably ruined by now. Those places don't provide ideal conditions for storing books."

"I'm sorry," she said, and for once, she meant it. She'd grown to love his collection of books almost as much as he did. They'd been her friends, her teachers and often her comfort. The thought of those books molding in a container somewhere made her heart hurt. "Maybe we can restore them. And find other copies of the ones you had to sell. I know it's not the same—"

"Where will we get the money?" Victor's eyebrows notched upward. "You see, I have a criminal record now. It's difficult to find a job."

"I don't have a record," she said, setting the can down on the counter, unopened. "I could help you. The way you helped me." She took a small measure of satisfaction in the double meaning in her words. She had every intention of helping Victor just as much as he'd helped her.

She'd help him back to prison the first chance he gave her.

Victor's eyes narrowed. "What are you really up to, Marisol? Why did you come back with me?"

She looked at him, trying to keep the fear out of her voice. "I'm trying to get back the best life I ever had."

"Marriage didn't suit you?"

She gave a huff of laughter, hoping she managed to infuse the right amount of disdain into the sound. "You were right. It was stifling. He wanted to control me, to keep me shackled to his bed. He rarely reads, has all the depth of a mud puddle and can't hold a conversation with a three-year-old."

A part of her felt sick for the lies she was telling about Jake. He was surprisingly well read for a man who made his living driving around a lake all day catching fish. He may not have shared his depth of character with her, but she'd seen it in so many unguarded moments and regretted her own choice to keep her heart and soul off limits to him.

And he could hold a marvelous conversation with a three-year-old. Her son Micah adored Jake.

Tears burned her eyes but she fought to keep them from falling. She had to sell this jaded disillusion to Victor with everything she had in her.

She had to give Jake a chance to escape and go for help.

But she suddenly realized, in a flash of certainty that threatened to shatter her careful control in front of Victor, that Jake would no more walk out of these woods than he'd dance naked on the streets of Gossamer Ridge.

Not while she was in danger.

It didn't matter whether or not he loved her. Jake wouldn't leave anyone in danger without trying to do something about it.

Sooner or later, he would show up here unarmed, injured and ready to fight Victor to the death to rescue her.

God help them all.

THE BELL 407 HELICOPTER was built to carry two crew and four passengers, but only Gabe and his brother J.D., a former navy helicopter pilot, were on the flight southwest to Buckley, Mississippi. The rain and wind forced them to hug the southern edge of the storm, adding a good thirty minutes to their flight schedule.

Gabe tried not to let panic set in.

About ten minutes into the flight, he'd gotten a call

from their younger brother, Aaron, a Chickasaw County Deputy, who'd received a bulletin from the Perry County Sheriff's Department. Power repair crews had happened across Jake's truck and boat partially submerged in the Leaf River just north of Beaumont, a town around forty-five minutes east of Buckley. No sign of Jake or Mariah, nor any of their clothes or personal effects. Just the truck and the boat. Perry County was dragging the truck out of the river and hoped to have more information after a closer examination.

"Can this bucket of rust go any faster?" he asked J.D.

J.D. slanted his brother a dark look. "I can't defy the laws of physics."

Gabe subsided against his seat, aware he was taxing his brother's short supply of patience where he was concerned. Not that he could blame J.D. for the constant tension between them, a disconnect that had festered for over more than years.

Hard to forgive a man who contributed to your wife's untimely death, even if he was your younger brother.

"We're half an hour out, maybe more if we keep having to detour around the storm. Might as well try to sit back and stop worrying about the things you can't change." J.D.'s voice filtered through the headphones, calm and flat.

Gabe couldn't tell if there was a double meaning in his brother's words, but it was hard not to read a bleak message into them anyway. Some things couldn't be changed, no matter how hard you tried. Especially not the past.

It could only be endured.

Against his side, his cell phone vibrated. He knew he'd never be able to hear anything over the roar of the helicopter's engine, but he checked the display. It was a text message from Kristen, his brother Sam's wife. "Check your email," it said.

He scanned the email message, his gut knotting pain-fully. "Kristen's talked to the Perry County Sheriff's Department. They said they received a bulletin from the next county over, trying to locate a missing conservation officer."

'   "What's that got to do with Jake and Mariah?"

"The officer was checking for storm damage near Buckley, Mississippi, when he disappeared," Gabe answered grimly. "Kristen got curious and looked up the last place the conservation officer had called in from before he went missing. Seems it's one of the two ways you can reach the interstate from Buckley. It's a longer route, so most people prefer to take the main highway."

"But maybe not right after a tornado when police are controlling access in and out of town?" J.D. guessed.

"Exactly." Gabe put the phone back in his pocket. "The cell tower Jake's phone pinged off of is about five miles from the access road. What are the odds that's a coincidence?"

J.D. glanced at him, his expression grim. "Pretty damned low, I reckon."

Gabe nodded. "Kristen's trying to get us clearing to land somewhere close to that point. She'll call back when she has something."

He just hoped they weren't too late.

JAKE FOUND THE ROAD quickly once he'd levered the tree off his leg, giving himself no breaks despite the pounding pain in his injured knee. He'd already lost fifteen minutes freeing himself from the fallen tree. He was damned lucky it hadn't taken longer.

It took him twenty minutes to walk the mile down the road to Victor's house, putting him over a half hour behind Victor and Mariah. A half hour was too long. Each minute had seemed to accumulate in the pit of his stomach, weighing him down until he dragged to a stop within sight of the house.

There was no good sheltered approach to the house, especially if Victor was on his guard, which he would have to be under these circumstances. And the direct approach would be a disaster—he was injured and unarmed, and Victor had a hostage.

And he couldn't be sure that the man with the rifle wouldn't ride in on his ATV to muck up everything.

The mystery man was the real wild card here, Jake knew. If Mariah's theory about Brenda's murder was right, then where did this guy fit in?

Jake hadn't gotten a look at the guy's face, but he was built like a young man. He gave off the impression of youth. Brenda had been murdered twelve years ago, hundreds of miles from here. Mariah had told him Victor had been a bit of a nomad in his younger days, moving from town to town in search of new adventures, taking jobs along the way.

But what about the younger man? He could have been in his mid-teens, maybe even younger. Even if he'd been capable of murder at that age, what were the odds he'd have been in Chickasaw County at that point in his life?

Don't get bogged down in what-ifs, he warned himself, trying to shake off the ache in his knee that shrouded his mind with pain. *Focus.*

He circled the house, keeping to the cover of the woods, until he reached the same corner from which he'd approached earlier that day. He doubted Victor had completely bought into Mariah's act, so he wouldn't have left her alone. They were likely to still be up in the front of the house.

Or maybe the basement, he realized, alarm flickering

through him at the memory of the shackles attached to the pipes.

Either way, he had a decent shot at making it to the house unnoticed the same way he had earlier that morning.

He reached the corner and waited a moment, listening. The last thing he was prepared to deal with was an ambush. But the woods around him were mostly silent. The earlier storm that had brought the pine tree down on his leg had subsided, replaced by a soaking rain, punctuated now and then by a gust of wind that rattled the treetops nearby.

Sunset was a couple of hours away, but the rain would hasten the darkness, giving Jake a decision to make. If he waited for the cover of twilight, he might have an even better angle of attack. But without knowing what was going on inside, he couldn't be sure how speedily he needed to act.

How long could Mariah feed Victor a load of bull before he'd stopped listening?

TOMATO SOUP BURBLED ON the stove eye, the sound soft and homey. The exact opposite of Mariah's emotional state.

Victor had settled down at the table, the small silver-barreled revolver sitting on the scarred tabletop in front of him. He fingered the ridges on the barrel, his gaze never leaving her as she stirred the soup.

"You know, there's going to be a lot of construction work going on, cleaning up after the storm." She wondered if a pot full of steaming tomato soup in Victor's face would slow him down enough for her to get away before he shot her again.

No, she decided. He was already on edge. He'd shoot her before she got the pot of soup anywhere near him.

"I thought of that already," Victor answered. "But I

won't be the only person out there competing for the jobs. And those other people won't be on parole."

"How did you manage parole, anyway?" As soon as she asked the question, Mariah realized she'd made a mistake. Out of the corner of her eye, she saw Victor's back stiffen.

"Would you have preferred I stayed there the rest of my life, I wonder?" His fingers tightened around the gun handle. She tried hard not to flinch. The more nervous she appeared, the tenser he'd get. She had to control herself, keep the atmosphere as light as possible until he finally dropped his guard enough for her to make a move.

A soft scraping sound from her right made her hand jerk. The wooden spoon she was using to stir the pot smacked against the side of the pan, making a loud thud.

Instinctively, she kept stirring, smacking her spoon against the pot to mask the furtive noises she heard coming from the direction of the mudroom.

Oh, Jake, what are you up to?

"Of course not," she answered, speaking in a firm, full voice, even though her insides were in a painful snarl. "I told you, I know the truth now. I just let my emotions tangle up my thinking. I can see so much more clearly now that I've had time to get past the experience and look at it logically." She turned to look at him, needing to reassure herself that he hadn't heard the sound of the window opening in the small alcove that led downstairs to the secret door in the basement.

He was looking at her, his dark eyes wistful. He really wanted to believe her, she realized, even though he knew full well that he'd murdered Micah Davis in cold blood.

He didn't want her to believe he was innocent because he cared what she thought of him, she knew. It was much more selfish than that. He wanted her to believe because it would cement his control of her. She'd be easier to manipulate if she were still the same, stupid girl she'd been when he first sucked her into his web all those years ago.

She turned back to the soup pot, listening for any more sounds from the back of the house. She heard nothing.

She wished she knew what Jake was planning. She could help him, keep Victor distracted, if she only knew what he was up to.

But all she could do was wait and pray she'd know what to do when the chance came.

She turned off the stove burner and looked at Victor. "It's ready. Should I spoon it up for you?"

Victor looked from the pot to her face and back. Suspicion gleamed in his eyes, making her glad she'd decided against trying to use the soup to incapacitate him. He'd have been ready for her, and she'd be dead.

Victor picked up the gun and flicked it at her. "Tell you what. I'll get you settled downstairs and then, after I eat, I'll bring you your dinner."

"Downstairs?" Her scalp prickled with alarm. Jake might be downstairs, with no place to hide. How quickly could he get to the secret door if he heard them coming? And even if he did, could he get out to the anteroom and close the hidden door behind him without Victor noticing?

"I can't leave you to your own devices, my dear." Victor stood, waiting for her to move ahead of him. She could see his patience was finite.

She walked slowly ahead of him, stumbling on purpose so that she made plenty of noise, in case Jake was downstairs, in need of a warning. She caught herself on the wall and glanced back at Victor, alarmed to find the snub-nosed revolver trained on her. "Sorry. I'm tired, and that makes me clumsy."

She reached the door to the basement and paused there, glancing back at Victor. "You know I'm afraid of basements," she said, loudly enough that Jake would surely hear if he were downstairs, hiding.

"You'll live," Victor said flatly, opening the door and giving her a nudge to go down the dark stairs first.

Quelling her old fears, she headed down the stairs, making as much noise as she could. She reached the bottom of the stairs, peering into the gloom for any sign that Jake was there.

Victor turned on the overhead bulb. Muddy yellow light cast an anemic glow in the center of the room, driving the shadows to the corners and recesses. Mariah looked around, her whole body wound as tight as a top, ready to spin out of control at the least provocation.

The basement was empty. Jake wasn't there.

A new thought struck her like ice water in her face.

What if it hadn't been Jake coming through the back window at all?

What if it was the man with the rifle?

Too close.

Jake's heart pounded so loudly he was half afraid that Victor could hear it on the other side of the hidden door. Fortunately, the sound of Mariah's voice, alerting him to their approach, had given him enough time to slip back out into the anteroom before they reached the bottom of the stairs.

The stone masonry stifled most of the noise coming from within the basement. He heard the muted sound of voices but couldn't make out any words.

Pressing his ear to the door, he tried to see if he could hear anything. The sounds grew deeper but no less garbled through the layers of wood and stone.

Damn it.

Why had Victor led her downstairs? He tried not to panic, his mind going through a number of unacceptable scenarios before he settled on the most obvious—Victor intended to chain her up in the shackles attached to the water pipes along the far wall. He couldn't allow her free access to his house; he couldn't trust her enough for that. Not yet. Probably never.

But he wasn't ready to kill her. If that's all he wanted, he'd have done it back in the woods, well away from his house, where there'd be less chance of incriminating evidence against him.

Jake comforted himself with that thought, hoping he wasn't just fooling himself.

If he'd brought her downstairs to chain her up, then he might not know that she and Jake had already found the escape hatch. Once he went upstairs, Jake could go back into the basement and free her, somehow. There had been all sorts of metal odds and ends lying around he could use to break the shackle locks, couldn't he?

A soft, furtive noise coming from above drew Jake's attention upward. He frowned, pressing his ear back to the hidden door. Had Victor already gone back upstairs?

He crept upstairs, his swollen knee howling with pain. He ignored it, pushing forward until he reached the top of the secret stairs and stepped into the laundry room.

Staying low, he risked a quick look outside the window. He saw nothing but rain drizzle and evidence of a lazy wind making the trees outside shiver and shimmy.

Another soft noise drew his attention, coming from the other side of the mudroom door.

Carefully, he closed his hand over the door handle, praying it wouldn't rattle when he tried the lock. He inched the knob to the right and felt more than heard the latch disengage.

Please don't creak.

The door swung into the mudroom, creating a harrowing blind spot. But if anyone was standing on the other side of the door, he already knew Jake was there, and there was nowhere to run even if he wanted to. The back door was padlocked shut, and Jake could never make it out of the laundry room window before whoever lurked outside could catch him.

He found the mudroom empty and released a silent breath, his nerves jangling with a combination of relief and letdown. Standing still and silent, he listened for more noise.

There. Coming from the kitchen.

There was no door to the mudroom, only a narrow archway. From where Jake stood, he could see only the side of the refrigerator. The table and stove were on the other side of the kitchen, out of sight.

He edged forward until he stood just inside the archway. Outside, the day was darkening to a deep grayish purple, turning the windows over the sink, just visible from Jake's position, into a mirror.

In the reflection, he saw the back of a man's head, bent over the stove. A head full of dark blond hair, the faint, peach-fuzz curve of a young man's jaw line, though Jake could make out little more about the man's features.

A moment later came the unmistakable hiss of gas from the stove eye.

The man turned from the stove, and Jake stepped back, not certain whether his own reflection might show in the kitchen window. He listened to the man's movements, the faint noise of socked feet moving across the floor. He'd taken pains to remove his shoes so he'd make no noise.

Did he already know Jake was inside the house? Was this an attempt to kill them all, maybe with a gas explosion? Clean up the mess once and for all?

The younger man's footsteps faded as he walked deeper into the house. Jake didn't dare follow him, knowing the rifle with the sound suppressor was surely standing nearby, ready for use.

Instead, he slipped back into the laundry room and shut the door behind him. He slid the window open, hoping the man would be too distracted by whatever plan he was putting into motion to hear the quiet sound. Then he descended the stairs again and paused in front of the secret door, listening.

He heard nothing.

Had Victor gone upstairs already? Jake heard nothing from the house above, so if Victor had gone back to the first floor, he hadn't happened across the mystery man yet.

Taking a deep breath, Jake decided to take the risk.

He pushed open the secret door and ducked inside.

Chapter Sixteen

Victor's footsteps hadn't made it all the way to the top of the stairs when Mariah heard the soft scrape of movement to her left. Peering into the shadows, she saw a shaft of light spread across the grimy basement floor.

Someone was coming through the secret door.

She peered up the steps, not sure whether to hope Victor hadn't heard or to pray he had. It all depended on who was coming through the door.

The door to the upstairs closed. Mariah turned back to the secret door.

It was closed. A tall, shadowy figure stood in the murky darkness in that corner of the room, blocked by a stack of ratty cardboard boxes from the reach of the overhead light.

The dark form moved toward her, stepping into the light.

Mariah's heart contracted.

"Are you okay?" Jake crossed to her, walking with an obvious limp.

"You got out," she whispered, her voice refusing to work.

He touched her face lightly, then glanced toward the stairs. "We have to get out of here."

"I know, but we're okay. I don't think he's coming back down here anytime soon."

"No, we've got to get out of here now." As he searched the basement for something to use to unlatch the handcuffs, Jake told her about seeing the mystery man tampering with the gas stove. "If he's planning on blowing this place up, we need to be out of here."

"My God." Mariah started tugging at the handcuffs, wondering if she could loosen the pipes and slip free that way. But the connections seemed solid.

"Here, let's see if this will work." Jake held a piece of wire he'd bent into a zigzag shape. He pushed the tip of the wire into the slot of the handcuffs. After a couple of twists and turns, the handcuff lock sprang open.

Mariah pulled off the cuff, rubbing her wrist. "Another secret deputy trick you learned?"

Jake shot her an amused look. "Remind me to tell you about my misspent youth." He wrapped his arm around her and started toward the secret door.

"What about Victor?" Mariah asked. "If that man is planning to blow this place up—"

Jake frowned, looking toward the top of the steps. "I don't know if we can risk it. He may shoot us before we get an explanation out."

Mariah knew he was right. She knew Victor would probably shoot Jake on sight this time. But despite all the terrible things he'd done, he'd still been good to her, in his own way, at a time when she needed someone to give a damn about whether or not she lived or died.

But she couldn't help him now. Whatever happened next, he'd brought it on himself.

"Let's go." Jake pulled her toward the secret door.

"No, wait! What about the binder?"

Jake paused mid-step, gazing at the stone wall where

they suspected the binder might be, temptation darkening his blue eyes. They both knew what a huge lead it might provide in the investigation of his sister-in-law's murder. But a second later, his mouth set in a resolute line. "No time. Let's go."

They took the steps as quietly as possible, determined not to draw attention if they could avoid it. But they also moved at a fast clip, uncertainty about what might happen next—and when—driving their steps.

The smell of gas wafted into the laundry room from the open mudroom door. Mariah heard Victor moving around in another part of the house, his movements quick and almost violent. "What is he doing?" she whispered.

"God only knows," Jake replied, using the cover of the noise Victor was making elsewhere to hide the sound of the window opening. The paint can Mariah had used to climb over the window sill was still on the laundry room floor. "Here, you first." Jake took her hand and helped her onto the can, giving her backside a nudge as she slipped through the window.

She landed hard on her uninjured side, the impact knocking her breath from her lungs for a second. She forced herself to breathe through the pain, pushing to her feet to help Jake out of the window behind her.

He tumbled out awkwardly, exhaling a low groan as he landed badly on the injured knee. He lay in the wet grass a second, gasping. "Go!" he urged her. "Get out of here."

She pulled him to his feet, ignoring the burn in her side, and wrapped her arm around his waist. "Not without my husband."

He managed to get his feet under him, pushing through obvious pain to keep pace with her as they ran for the woods.

They made it past the first palisade of trees before a

concussive explosion rocked the ground beneath their feet. Jake pushed Mariah to the forest floor, covering her body with his. Though debris rained around them, the dense mass of spring growth acted as an umbrella, sparing them from injury.

Jake pushed to his feet, turning to look behind them. Mariah unfolded herself and joined him, staring at the mass of flames that had once been Victor's house.

"Maybe the binder will be protected by the stone wall," Mariah murmured, reading his mind in his pained expression. "We might still get something out of it."

"Maybe," he murmured, turning away. She could tell he didn't have much hope.

"Wonder if the van made it through the explosion?" Mariah tugged Jake's hand, pulling him toward the front of the house. But her nascent hope of driving out of the woods was dashed at the sight of the van lying on its side where the blast had knocked it. Even if they were able to right it, Mariah doubted it was safe to drive.

"I guess we'll have to walk out," Jake said quietly. "But we should stick to the woods. I don't know where our mystery man went. We'd be sitting ducks out in the open."

Mariah knew he was right, though the thought of trekking through the viny undergrowth for God knew how many miles held no appeal for her after all they'd been through. But it was the only way out.

Squeezing his hand, she followed him into the woods.

GABE'S SISTER-IN-LAW Kristen had talked the local sheriff's department into letting the Bell 407 land on the roof heliport at the department's complex, an arrangement the Buckley sheriff had agreed to once he realized the missing driver of the recovered truck and boat was an Alabama lawman. Gabe and J.D. were about twenty minutes from the sheriff's department, flying over a densely forested area, when Gabe spotted a bright glow in the middle of the expanse of green.

He nudged J.D. "What is that?"

J.D.'s wide forehead creased. "Forest fire?"

"After all this rain?" Something about the flickering yellow blaze sent a shudder through Gabe. The back of his neck prickled. "Is there anywhere to put down around here?"

J.D. swung the bird a little north, taking a wide sweep over the area. A few minutes later, Gabe spotted a narrow gray thread running through the greenery. And not far from that, a less defined brown track indicated a second road, winding into the forest proper. It seemed to lead back toward the burning area in the heart of the woods.

"That's a road," Gabe said, pointing to the gray strip. "And it seems to turn off onto a smaller road leading toward the fire. Can we get closer?"

J.D. nodded, dropping the helicopter's altitude as they approached the road. There was still enough daylight left to see that what had looked like a gray strip from above was a paved two-lane road, stretching several miles in either direction. It intersected with a dirt road that seemed to wind deep into the heart of the woods.

J.D. nodded toward the road. "If I'm reading our maps right, isn't that the road where they found the conservation officer's body? We're a few miles from that point, but I think it's the same road—"

"Can you put this bird down there?"

A slow grin spread across J.D.'s wide mouth. "Can a Cooper catch a fish?"

THE SOUND OF A HELICOPTER overhead broke through the haze of pain dogging Jake's every step. Looking toward what sky was visible through the trees overhead, he tried to spot the craft.

"Sounds close." Mariah's breath warmed the side of his neck. She was taking the brunt of their combined weight, half holding him up as he hobbled through the woods, barely keeping his feet as they stumbled through the underbrush, moving slowly, inexorably toward the main road.

The underside of the helicopter flashed white above them as the craft made a lazy circle overhead, then dipped lower. Was it going to land nearby?

"I think they're landing!" Mariah's grip around his waist tightened and she urged him to pick up his pace.

They had stayed off the dirt road all the way out of the woods, not just because of the mystery man who'd set the gas explosion but also because they couldn't be sure Victor hadn't gotten out of the house before the blast. If either man found them this time, they'd kill them. Jake had no doubt.

But if that helicopter dropping in for a landing on the road just north could offer the rescue they sought, then it was worth the risk taking the fastest route out of the woods. He guided Mariah toward the dirt road.

They had been hiking parallel to the dirt track for miles now. They should be getting close to the main road, if the sound of the descending helicopter was anything to go by.

They reached the dirt track a couple of minutes later and started down the muddy road. It was lined by trees on either side that blocked their view of the main road ahead. But the thudding roar of the landing helicopter was loud and getting louder with each step.

Suddenly, the helicopter noise died. The silence felt like a living thing, filling Jake's ears and winding its way through his weary brain. Someone had shut off the helicopter engine. They were probably getting out to walk.

Mariah tucked closer. "What if it's the man with the rifle?" she breathed, her voice barely a whisper.

The back of Jake's neck began to prickle. He couldn't explain why, but he was certain whoever was in the helicopter was a friend, not a foe. "It's not," he said with confidence that surprised even him.

They heard voices ahead, though they couldn't make out any words. Mariah slowed her steps, curling her hand into Jake's palm. "Wait—"

The dirt track curved just ahead. The voices they were hearing grew more audible. A couple of seconds later, the speakers came around the clump of trees that had formerly blocked them from view. Two men, both tall, though one towered over the other. Dark hair. Trim, athletic builds.

And one of them had a face that, for Jake, was like looking into a mirror.

"Oh, my God," Mariah breathed beside him, her voice little more than air.

Gabe and J. D. Cooper froze for a second, staring down the road at them as if not certain what they were seeing. Then Gabe broke into a run.

Jake hobbled toward his twin brother, a bubble of pure, joyous relief swelling in his chest until it burst.

The cavalry had finally arrived.

"THE COPS LOOKED WHERE you told them, but the place is pretty far gone. They did find something hidden in the walls, but most of the pages are burned to ash. They're looking to see if they can get something more out of the pieces that weren't as badly damaged, but it's not going to be a high priority for the Mississippi State Crime Lab." Gabe directed his words to Jake, but his gaze slid sideways toward J.D., who sat, entirely too silent, in a chair next to Jake's hospital bed.

"I was afraid that might be the case." Jake reached over and touched J.D.'s arm. "I'm sorry, man. I couldn't go back for it. I had to get Mariah out of there."

J.D.'s blue eyes met Jake's. He saw pain in his eldest brother's eyes, but also understanding. "You did the right thing. Of course."

"It's still a lead," Jake pointed out. "Somewhere new to look that we didn't have before."

"I can't believe Mariah sat on this the whole time," Gabe murmured. "Hell, I can't believe she had a whole secret life—"

"I'm really sorry about that."

At the sound of Mariah's voice, all three men turned to look at the door, where she stood, wrapped in an oversized hospital gown, her arms hugging herself as if she were cold.

"May I come in?" she asked.

"Of course," Jake said firmly, his heart contracting at the sight of her guilt and shame. He understood her so much better now than he had even a few days earlier, felt her sense of regret as deeply as his own.

And in the last couple of days, he'd discovered that he loved her in a way he'd never thought he could love anyone in the world. The thought was as terrifying as it was wonderful.

Because there was every chance, every probability, that she would never love him the same way.

"The police had a lot of questions about Victor," she said, walking slowly toward the bed. "I told them everything I knew. I promise." She'd directed the last statement toward J.D., who was watching her with wary eyes.

"You should have told us," he said in a low, pained voice.

"I know. I wasn't sure. And I didn't want to send you on another wild-goose chase without proof." She smiled her thanks at Gabe, who'd pulled up the extra chair so she could sit next to Jake's bed. "I'm sorry."

"I need to call home, make sure the family has an update on what's going on." J.D. pushed to his feet, towering over Jake's bed. Jake reached out and caught his brother's hand, holding him in place for a moment.

"Thanks for the rescue. I don't know how you found us—"

"Ask your twin." J.D. gave Jake's hand a quick squeeze, then he was gone, out the hospital room door in a few long strides.

"He'll understand eventually," Jake promised Mariah.

"Yeah, good luck," Gabe murmured, his voice dark with regret. Jake knew how much his twin blamed himself for Brenda's death. He'd tried to convince Gabe that one stupid mistake—letting the time slip away from him, making him late picking her up from work when her car wouldn't start—could have happened to anyone. On any other night, it would have been nothing.

But it hadn't happened any other night. It had happened the night a vicious killer had caught Brenda coming out of the trucking company, where she had been working a night shift alone, and murdered her.

Gabe had arrived in time to find her body still warm.

Gabe put his hand on Jake's shoulder. "Listen, I've got to get out of here, too. I promised Hannah I'd call and let her know all the details, and I don't want to call so late I wake up the little cowpoke."

"Give her my love."

"Oh, she'll expect you to do that yourself the minute

you're out of this joint." Gabe started to leave, then turned back, looking at Mariah. "None of this changes anything, Mariah. You know that, right? You're still a Cooper."

Mariah's eyes glistened with tears. "Thank you." The words came out strangled with emotion.

Gabe waved at Jake, and then he was gone, too, closing the door behind him.

"I think he just wanted to give us time alone," Jake said quietly, smiling a little as Mariah turned to look at him. "He always could read my mind."

"You're probably tired. I should go—"

He caught her hand before she could rise. "I think we need to talk, don't you?"

Before she could speak, the phone on Jake's bedside table rang. He frowned at the interruption, but Mariah picked up the phone and answered.

It was his mother. "We're both going to be fine, Beth," Mariah assured her, glancing at Jake, a faint smile curving her lips. "My wound is half healed, and I'll let Jake tell you about his knee." She handed over the phone. "Your mom."

"Yes, just a very bad bruise. And it was hyperextended in the fall, so there's some strain on the ligaments and tendons, but nothing's torn or broken. I should be getting out of this joint tomorrow." Jake caught Mariah's hand so she couldn't leave while he was on the phone. "How's Micah?"

"He's doing fine. Just misses you both terribly," Beth Cooper replied.

Mariah leaned closer at the mention of her son's name. "Is he awake?" she whispered.

"Is he awake? Could we talk to him?" Jake asked his mother.

His mother handed the phone over to Micah, who

babbled excitedly at the sound of Jake's voice. Jake could make out maybe three or four words amid the noise the exuberant three-year-old was making—something about a dog and cake.

"Let me," Mariah said, her voice urgent. Jake handed her the phone.

"Hey, baby. It's Mommy." As she talked to her son, a smile lit Mariah's features as if she'd stepped into sunlight. Jake's chest swelled at the sight of her beautiful face, so familiar in some ways, so wonderfully different in others. Had she really hidden this open, emotional woman from him for almost three years? Or had he simply refused to see her, knowing what a threat she'd pose to his carefully guarded heart?

"We'll be home soon, baby. Mama loves you."

"Daddy loves you, too," Jake added, taking the phone to say goodbye to the little boy he thought of as his own. A second later, his mother came on the phone to say goodbye as well. Finally, Jake handed the phone back to Mariah. She hung it up and turned slowly back to face him.

"You wanted to talk." She sounded as if she had to force the words between her lips.

"Things have changed." At the look of fear in her eyes, he realized he'd started bluntly, so he added, "Not for the worse."

She started to sit back in the chair, but Jake patted the bed beside him. Carefully, she perched on the edge of the bed, looking down at him, her eyes wary.

Jake decided this conversation wasn't something he could ease into. So he got straight to the point. "I love you. More than I realized I could. I think it took seeing the real you to get me over that hump, but whatever caused it, it's true. I love you. I just need to know if you think you'll ever be able to love me, too."

The stunned look on her face made his stomach knot. "You said you didn't even know who I am."

"I didn't. I do now." He managed a smile, though his face felt as if it were about to break. "Run for your life through the woods with a person, you get to know them pretty well."

She made a small huffing noise that might have been a laugh. But her eyes welled with tears, suggesting the sound might have been a sob instead. "This isn't exactly what I was expecting from this conversation."

"I didn't see the point of tiptoeing around the bottom line," Jake said, reaching out to take her hand. "Can you fall in love with me?"

Her gaze lifted from their entwined hands to meet his eyes. "Already done."

His heart gave an odd flop at the look in those quicksilver eyes. "Don't say that because you think you have to."

"I'm not." Her voice was soft and raspy, but a thread of steel ran through it. "Remember, I'm the one who saw who you really are a long time before you figured it out. I think I've loved you all along. I just wouldn't let myself call it that."

"Because it would feel like cheating on Micah's father?"

She nodded. "It was hard to believe I could have anything as good as what Micah and I had again. I couldn't let myself think that way."

"What about now?"

She smiled at him, the light back, spreading a golden glow over him that made his chest hurt with its beauty. She bent toward him, her hair spilling over him like an inky waterfall. "Now, I really want to kiss my husband."

And she did.

Epilogue

It took a little doing to talk the doctors at the Hattiesburg hospital into letting them leave with Gabe and J.D. after only one night in the hospital. Mariah's temperature was still hovering around 99 degrees, and Jake's badly sprained knee was swollen to the size of a grapefruit. But the doctors finally relented, full of disapproval, signing the release papers around one. By three the next day, the Bell 407 was in the air, aimed east toward Alabama.

The Buckley authorities still had a lot to sort out about the events of the past few days, but a phone call from Jake's brother Aaron at the Chickasaw County Sheriff's Department had reassured the Buckley cops that Jake and Mariah would be available for any further questions that might arise.

They'd learned, just before leaving town, that Victor's body had been thrown clear of the fire by the initial explosion. Searchers found him about thirty feet away, his neck snapped. Positive ID—Victor was dead.

Mariah wasn't sure whether to feel relieved or sad.

The deputies were still hunting for the man with the rifle. She and Jake hadn't been able to give them much of a description, unfortunately. They'd never seen his face.

J.D. and Gabe were in the cockpit, leaving Mariah and Jake alone in the belly of the helicopter, although the open body design gave them nothing like privacy. Still, Mariah took advantage of their turned backs to reach up and kiss the underside of Jake's jaw.

"Are you trying to kill me?" he asked in a low groan she could barely hear over the engine, his breath hot against her cheek.

"Don't even joke about that." She rubbed her face against his, the memories of the last few days sending a shudder through her. "If something had happened, if Victor had killed you—"

"He didn't."

"He could have." Ignoring the sharp twinge in her injured side, she shifted her position in the seat to look into his calm blue eyes. The openness that greeted her there was so new, so precious, that tears pricked her own eyes. "I love you. You know that, don't you?"

He touched her face, his fingers moving lightly over the curve of her cheek. "I know." He kissed her again.

The sound of the helicopter engine shifted, gearing down. Mariah dragged her mouth away from Jake to look out the window. Gossamer Lake spread out to the west, reflecting the clear blue sky like a sparkling jewel. They were close to touching down at the Chickasaw County Aviation helipad.

The helicopter landed with a light thud, and Jake released Mariah's hand so that he could remove his seatbelt. The engine died down to nothing and the door opened from the outside, revealing half the Cooper family there to greet them. Jake's brother Luke, who made his own hours at the stable he ran, was there, along with their sister Hannah, a fishing guide and Mariah's boss at the family marina office.

Both of Jake's parents had made the trip to the heliport as well, and it didn't take long for Beth Cooper, who'd spent her younger years as a registered nurse, to whisk Mariah aside to check her over. "Temp seems to be coming down. Good sign." She checked Mariah's pulse. "Good and strong. I always told Jake you looked like you came from tough people." She smiled.

Mariah realized there were a whole lot of Coopers who'd have to learn the full truth about her background. She sought Jake among the family members milling about the heliport, spotting him standing off to one side, talking to his father.

"Beth, I need to talk to Jake a minute. I'll bring him over here to let you take a look at him, too, I promise." She squeezed her mother-in-law's hand and hurried to Jake's side.

He was favoring his bad knee, she noted, his arm around his father's shoulder to stay upright. "You should find a place to sit down," she said quietly.

Mike Cooper waved toward the dark-green SUV parked in the lot nearby. "Think you can get to the car on your own? I'll go fetch your mother to take a look at your knee."

Mariah led Jake to the SUV, helping him into the middle of the vehicle. "What are you thinking?" Jake asked, his hand lingering, soft and warm, against the back of her neck.

"I was thinking about Victor," she admitted. "He had so much he could have offered the world, you know? If he'd been a different person. I mean, he was smart and persistent and—" She paused, surprised to find that the strongest emotion she felt right now about Victor's death was sadness. "But I guess he was just too damaged to ever be fixed."

Jake didn't look sad, just angry. "Victor earned the end he got, baby. Don't mourn what he could have been. He chose to embrace the damage rather than rise above it, the way you did."

She laughed without mirth. "I don't know that I've risen above it. Look at the mess I made of us."

"You had help." He brushed his thumb across her lower lip, his gaze dipping to follow its path. "But we're going to fix that, right?"

She smiled, some of the melancholy lifting as she saw the blaze of emotion in his eyes when they rose to meet hers.

"I feel like such a fool for being afraid of this." His thumb slid downward until he cupped her chin with his palm.

"Of what?"

"Of loving someone as much as I love you." He bent and kissed her, the touch almost reverent.

She wrapped her arms around him and rose into the kiss, answering his reverence with a passion she'd kept in check too long. As he pulled her closer, deepening the kiss, the world around them faded into a shimmering cloud of beautiful nothingness.

We're going to be okay, she told herself.

And this time, she finally believed it.

* * * * *

Don't miss
THE MAN FROM GOSSAMER RIDGE
as Paula Graves's
COOPER JUSTICE: COLD CASE INVESTIGATION
continues. Look for it
wherever Harlequin Intrigue books are sold!

Harlequin®

INTRIGUE®

COMING NEXT MONTH

Available May 10, 2011

#1275 BABY BOOTCAMP
Daddy Corps
Mallory Kane

#1276 BRANDED
Whitehorse, Montana: Chisholm Cattle Company
B.J. Daniels

#1277 DAMAGED
Colby Agency: The New Equalizers
Debra Webb

#1278 THE MAN FROM GOSSAMER RIDGE
Cooper Justice: Cold Case Investigation
Paula Graves

#1279 UNFORGETTABLE
Cassie Miles

#1280 BEAR CLAW CONSPIRACY
Bear Claw Creek Crime Lab
Jessica Andersen

You can find more information on upcoming
Harlequin® titles, free excerpts and more at
www.HarlequinInsideRomance.com.

HICNM0411

REQUEST YOUR FREE BOOKS!
2 FREE NOVELS PLUS 2 FREE GIFTS!

ⓢ Harlequin®

INTRIGUE®

BREATHTAKING ROMANTIC SUSPENSE

YES! Please send me 2 FREE Harlequin Intrigue® novels and my 2 FREE gifts (gifts are worth about $10). After receiving them, if I don't wish to receive any more books, I can return the shipping statement marked "cancel." If I don't cancel, I will receive 6 brand-new novels every month and be billed just $4.24 per book in the U.S. or $4.99 per book in Canada. That's a saving of at least 15% off the cover price! It's quite a bargain! Shipping and handling is just 50¢ per book in the U.S. and 75¢ per book in Canada.* I understand that accepting the 2 free books and gifts places me under no obligation to buy anything. I can always return a shipment and cancel at any time. Even if I never buy another book, the two free books and gifts are mine to keep forever.

182/382 HDN FC5H

Name	(PLEASE PRINT)

Address	Apt. #

City	State/Prov.	Zip/Postal Code

Signature (if under 18, a parent or guardian must sign)

Mail to the **Reader Service:**
IN U.S.A.: P.O. Box 1867, Buffalo, NY 14240-1867
IN CANADA: P.O. Box 609, Fort Erie, Ontario L2A 5X3

Not valid for current subscribers to Harlequin Intrigue books.

**Are you a subscriber to Harlequin Intrigue books
and want to receive the larger-print edition?
Call 1-800-873-8635 or visit www.ReaderService.com.**

* Terms and prices subject to change without notice. Prices do not include applicable taxes. Sales tax applicable in N.Y. Canadian residents will be charged applicable taxes. Offer not valid in Quebec. This offer is limited to one order per household. All orders subject to credit approval. Credit or debit balances in a customer's account(s) may be offset by any other outstanding balance owed by or to the customer. Please allow 4 to 6 weeks for delivery. Offer available while quantities last.

Your Privacy—The Reader Service is committed to protecting your privacy. Our Privacy Policy is available online at www.ReaderService.com or upon request from the Reader Service.

We make a portion of our mailing list available to reputable third parties that offer products we believe may interest you. If you prefer that we not exchange your name with third parties, or if you wish to clarify or modify your communication preferences, please visit us at www.ReaderService.com/consumerschoice or write to us at Reader Service Preference Service, P.O. Box 9062, Buffalo, NY 14269. Include your complete name and address.

HI11

*With an evil force hell-bent on destruction,
two enemies must unite to find a truth that turns
all-too-personal when passions collide.*

*Enjoy a sneak peek in Jenna Kernan's next installment
in her original* TRACKER *series, GHOST STALKER,
available in May, only from Harlequin Nocturne.*

"**W**ho are you?" he snarled.

Jessie lifted her chin. "Your better."

His smile was cold. "Such arrogance could only come from a Niyanoka."

She nodded. "Why are you here?"

"I don't know." He glanced about her room. "I asked the birds to take me to a healer."

"And they have done so. Is that *all* you asked?"

"No. To lead them away from my friends." His eyes fluttered and she saw them roll over white.

Jessie straightened, preparing to flee, but he roused himself and mastered the momentary weakness. His eyes snapped open, locking on her.

Her heart hammered as she inched back.

"Lead who away?" she whispered, suddenly afraid of the answer.

"The ghosts. Nagi sent them to attack me so I would bring them to her."

The wolf must be deranged because Nagi did not send ghosts to attack living creatures. He captured the evil ones after their death if they refused to walk the Way of Souls, forcing them to face judgment.

"Her? The healer you seek is also female?"

"Michaela. She's Niyanoka, like you. The last Seer of Souls and Nagi wants her dead."

Jessie fell back to her seat on the carpet as the possibility of this ricocheted in her brain. Could it be true?

"Why should I believe you?" But she knew why. His black aura, the part that said he had been touched by death. Only a ghost could do that. But it made no sense.

Why would Nagi hunt one of her people and why would a Skinwalker want to protect her? She had been trained from birth to hate the Skinwalkers, to consider them a threat.

His intent blue eyes pinned her. Jessie felt her mouth go dry as she considered the impossible. Could the trickster be speaking the truth? Great Mystery, what evil was this?

She stared in astonishment. There was only one way to find her answers. But she had never even met a Skinwalker before and so did not even know if they dreamed.

But if he dreamed, she would have her chance to learn the truth.

*Look for GHOST STALKER by Jenna Kernan,
available May only from Harlequin Nocturne,
wherever books and ebooks are sold.*

Harlequin® *Romance*

Don't miss an irresistible new trilogy
from acclaimed author

SUSAN MEIER

IN THE BOARDROOM

Greek Tycoons become devoted dads!

Coming in April 2011

The Baby Project

Whitney Ross is terrified when she becomes guardian
to a tiny baby boy, but everything changes when
she meets dashing Darius Andreas, Greek tycoon
and now a brand-new daddy!

Second Chance Baby (*May 2011*)
Baby on the Ranch (*June 2011*)

www.eHarlequin.com

HR17721